DEVON C. FORD

AFTERMATH

TOY SOLDIERS

AETHON BOOKS

AFTERMATH

©2019 DEVON C. FORD

Print and eBook formatting, and cover design by Steve Beaulieu.

Published by Aethon Books LLC. 2019

All characters in this book are fictitious. Any resemblance to actual persons, living or dead, is purely coincidental.

Dedicated to SC.

Defying modern medicine at every turn and thriving on sheer stubbornness.

ALSO IN THE SERIES

Toy Soldiers:

Apocalypse

Aftermath

Abandoned

Adversity

Books five and six yet to be named (coming 2019)

PREFACE

All spelling and grammar in this book is UK English except for proper nouns and those American terms which just don't anglicize.

PROLOGUE

"Sir, I have Castlemartin on the horn now," said the radio operator in a distinctly southern states accent. The way he pronounced the name, *Cassulmart'n*, was an assault on the ears of Commander Ethan Briggs of Her Majesty's Royal Navy.

The 'Sir' being addressed wasn't Briggs, he was merely there as liaison to the United States Navy, having been transported by one of the two Sea King helicopters belonging to the American destroyer. It had been sailing back from active service in the Persian Gulf, where it had been patrolling as protection for the oil drilling operation and found itself diverted to a crisis with infinitely further-reaching consequences than petty squabbles over natural resources.

"Okay, apprise them of our situation and request that they monitor this channel for orders," came the steady, almost flat voice of the ship's captain.

Briggs, as much as he hated the way they pronounced Castlemartin, breathed a small sigh of relief that nobody had referred to the area by its county of Pembrokeshire. Twice he had been on the inexplicable verge of raging at the American crewman on the radio for saying it as three distinctly clear and separate syllables of *Pem-Broke-Shire* as though the place was a village in a Tolkien novel.

"Commander Briggs?" the captain asked politely. "How are we set?"

Briggs checked his watch and flicked his eyes back to the pad in front of him before answering.

"Sir, there is no way the convoy can make it back in time without assistance," he responded, seeing the captain merely nod and keep his eyes facing resolutely forward at the distant shoreline of south western Britain, as if his vision could detect this new and unfathomable enemy.

He turned back to the radio operator again to ask, "Are the air assets a go or not?"

The man looked up from the control panel he was staring at in that curious way people did to hear better.

"Negative, Sir," he said sternly, making Briggs wonder whether the concept of melodrama had been an entirely American invention, "Harrier strike group still engaged on the continent."

"Well, shi-it," the captain said, drawing out the word into two long syllables, "Crewman, send in the tanks."

Briggs' eyes met the captain's.

"Never thought I'd ever give that order," he said with a rueful smile. The crewman manning the radio nodded once and answered, "Aye, aye, Sir," before chattering into the microphone.

Briggs felt an overwhelming sense of dread at potentially having to use up that resource, but he saw no other way to ensure the success of the mission.

The swarm was still out of range of their guns, the use of cruise missile strikes had been vetoed at the highest level, despite assurances of their accuracy, and they had no chance of a rescue by helicopter without abandoning almost every man in the convoy and exposing their precious cargo to hazards beyond their control.

That helicopter rescue was still an option, but it was a last ditch attempt that wasn't their call to make.

It was a plan that Briggs didn't want to consider using, as it would mean the deaths of more than thirty men that his plan had placed in harm's way.

Damned if they do, Briggs told himself, *and damned if they don't... but I rather suspect we are all damned.*

ONE

"Wind right to left, gentle," said the mound of green and brown brush behind Marine Enfield in a low voice, "distance six-hundred yards."

"Six-fifteen," Enfield muttered back, his right eye not leaving the large scope on top of his Accuracy International, or L96a, sniper rifle. His right hand moved on muscle memory, making the finite adjustments as he clicked the dials on the big optic, all the while keeping the target in sight. They were far enough away that the likelihood of being detected by the sound of the impending gunshot was small, but still they couldn't risk not relocating after taking out a target.

The teamwork displayed by the two marines, Craig Enfield being the shooter and Martin Leigh his spotter, was exceptional and spoke of the many hours they had spent together in uncomfortable silence and danger. They had both missed out, as they saw it, on seeing deployment to the Falklands seven years before, as they'd still been in their first year of training together, but the pair had seen more than enough of the green landscape and streets of Northern Ireland.

Now, instead of their enemy being terrorist bombers or

shooters, instead of being the mighty steel boot of the Soviet Union stamping towards Europe, an enemy they had been training for years to combat should the Cold War turn hot, they were now stalking zombies.

Screechers, as the army lot had called them, and it had stuck as a name they used for them, mostly because when the things detected you, they let out a squealing hissing, ripping noise. They didn't know if it was excitement or, more frighteningly, a call to other zombies to advertise the presence of food, but they did know it was a fucking awful sound that stopped if you stuck a bayonet through their eye.

"I've got it," Enfield said, in a cool murmur as the reticule of his scope hovered just above and to the left of the head of the Screecher.

"Zero, this is Whisky," Leigh said softly into his radio, "we have a Lima in sight, over."

———

Limas. The military's pathological need to provide a nickname or a phonetic tag for something ran deeper than the coded letter and number designations they gave to all of their weapons and equipment. Lima meant a fast one, the *Leaders* as they had been dubbed. Until the Marines had landed in their helicopter on the small island a fraction off the south coast, they hadn't encountered one of these before.

Studies of their new and unexpected enemy had shown that they operated some kind of biologically determined rank structure of their own, and each Leader would somehow gather up to a hundred Screechers who followed them around like ducklings. The Leaders weren't just faster, they were smarter too. Some reckoned they could open doors, and there was even an emerging theory among the joint army, navy and marine forces that they had some way to give orders to their followers.

Those followers were deadly in numbers, but on their own weren't too difficult to kill. A heavy blow to the head, one strong enough to crack the skull, would usually render them inert, but that kind of swing burned a lot of energy and anyone trying to survive out there using a sledgehammer would find themselves tiring too quickly, and probably being eaten. The careful application of bayonet to brain was far more civilised, but a bullet would do the trick just as easily. The problem with bullets, especially the heavy ammunition that the RMPs 7.62mm SLRs or Self-Loading Rifles fired, was that they tended to be accompanied by lots of noise.

Noise, especially gunfire, carried a long way and noise was what attracted the Screechers like flies to shit.

Another theory about the Screechers was that they were blind, or at least had very poor eyesight, because anyone who had seen one up close reported the dead look in their cloudy eyes.

But noise was what got people killed. It was what attracted them to group together, as one stumbling zombie would knock into something and attract another nearby zombie to the noise. Those small noises they made would keep them clumped into a group, and each group of any more than a dozen of them almost always had a Lima in the middle of them, ready to break out and run at anything still living. The reverse characteristic of that strange attraction they had was that when the Lima got taken out, the Screechers tended to bumble around until other noises caught their attention and they simply wandered off to find more groups or get stuck somewhere on their own.

Three times there had been reports of mass-gatherings, or swarms as they had been called. The early warning plane that the Americans had been flying over the UK at an altitude so high that it couldn't be detected by the naked eye or ear, had watched these swarms gather, reporting that on two occasions those massed crowds had simply dissipated, as though the Screechers had lost interest or the noise they made collectively was simply too confusing and overwhelming to hold their attention.

The third swarm, luckily as they had later discovered, was the smallest by far, and it had gathered and massed in their direction as the sound of an armoured convoy had attracted them after more than one rolling battle. The small cannons and heavy machine guns of the Yeomanry had taken a devastating toll on the army of the dead, but they had made too much noise in doing so, and brought every infected corpse within a fifty-mile radius directly to their doorway.

The marines of 40 Commando, deployed to protect the assets of 3 Commando Brigade Air Squadron who flew the attack helicopters, had been splintered off from their main group and hastily ordered into two Sea Kings from the naval airbase they were defending.

Their most senior command, seemingly being run from the huge flagship aircraft carrier floating in the channel, had issued the squad of marines, some of whom had been volunteered for the ground convoy bringing supplies and fuel for the two helicopters, with orders to reinforce the light tanks and await further orders. Apparently, command had decided that the only intact armour squadron on mainland Britain deserved a sprinkling of Royal Marines to add flavour and diversity, not to mention adding some firepower to complement the aircraft.

Of the suspected inter-services rivalry, there had been precisely none. No man in his right mind would think to raise an objection at being given an order by an Admiral instead of a General, given their current and unprecedented situation, nor would marines on the ground show disobedience to the officers and NCOs of the army unit.

orders and I will deal with you another time," he ordered him. The man half-turned to his right, stamped his boot loudly and marched away, demonstrating parade-ground drill precision. Johnson turned back to his own man, who shrank slightly.

"Trooper Nevin," Johnson said in a voice scarce above a whisper, "I can only assume, having never met the man, that your father wished you had been a wank. You, trooper Nevin, are a five-foot-six walking advert for condoms!"

Nevin said nothing, but swallowed nervously. The insults had been designed to prompt a laugh from him, daring him to smirk when lined up in the SSM's sights, but the man clearly had some love for life left in him, so he kept very quiet.

"Stand at ease," he told him, seeing the man relax, "you are also confined to barracks until such time as I decide exactly how angry I am with you; because at the moment it would be inhumane to do half of what I'm thinking." He stepped back and drew himself up formally.

"Detail," he snapped, prompting the ingrained habit of any soldier to tense in anticipation of the next order, "atteeeeenSHUN!" Johnson ordered. Just as Nevin's right leg rose to a ninety-degree angle and stopped to stamp back down to the street, Johnson's large right fist shot out and upwards, burying itself deep in Nevin's diaphragm and doubling him over to leave him gasping on the ground to draw in enough breath to vomit the single pint of bitter he had been permitted.

"Dismissed," Johnson said casually as he walked back towards the command post.

From the shadows a short distance away, two marines with an intrinsic understanding of one another smiled as they watched the trooper writhing about in pain. They were a pair, a duo, inseparable since they had joined on the same intake to undergo one of the hardest military selection processes imaginable, and their bond of friendship had grown even more unbreakable when they had attended the marksman training course where the shooter and his spotter were hardened into a devilishly sharp weapon to be used against the enemies of Her Majesty.

———

"Permission to engage the Lima?" asked Leigh into the radio, then waited as he listened to the response, before slowly moving the strong binoculars back up to his eyes.

"All yours," he said quietly to his shooter, who lay just ahead of him and to his left, "fire when rea…"

A booming report erupted from just ahead of him, making him reacquire the Lima in his binoculars in time to see it lie flat on its back. It was all but headless. Taking his eyes away, he saw the slow and controlled movements of Enfield as his right hand carefully lifted and drew back the bolt of the rifle to eject the spent brass and collect it smoothly with his index and middle fingers. Racking the bolt quickly would eject the casing to spin it out away from the breech to twinkle in the light, and that might reveal their position to an enemy sniper or, more appropriately in their current setting, attract the attention of a hungry walking corpse. The sniper's natural inclination towards silence and invisibility was a skill that couldn't be taught, but it could be honed.

"Lima rendered safe," Leigh reported emotionlessly over the radio.

Enfield slipped the empty casing into a pouch on his webbing, flicked the safety catch on his big rifle and offered his opinion on what they should do next.

"Time to move," he said, "before any of the fuckers decide to investigate where that came from."

TWO

In the few weeks since the bizarre battle of the bridge, where the tanks had advanced into the boiling mass of bodies to crush a wide swathe flat and render them safe, an air of something resembling business as usual had descended over the island. 'Rendering them safe' had become the adopted terminology, as it was technically inaccurate to report that they had killed them, or killed them *again,* and it helped them come to terms with what they had to do on an almost daily basis.

As inhuman and inhumane as the Screechers were, they had still been innocent people once. Looking down the barrel of a gun at one revealed the close-up secrets that a person chose not to see when fear gripped them, and those details showed their clothes and gave hints of their former lives. The shorter ones especially had to be de-humanised in the minds of the living, as to acknowledge what they were would be to accept the killing of a child. An *innocent* child. That was one of the reasons the terminology was first coined and why people had taken to it so easily. Nobody wanted to report that they had killed a child but reporting that they had rendered them safe sounded like the mercy it truly was.

The battle of the bridge had seen the unexpected arrival of the helicopters and the jaw-dropping display they had treated everyone to. This was coupled with the most bizarre antics of the crew chief of one of the aircraft, who had rigged a massive speaker from their mess to work as a noise lure, as if the spinning blades and screaming whine of the engines wouldn't be enough. The amazing appearance of the helicopters that day had become a daily reminder that the people and forces of Britain were scattered and forced to come together in unprecedented ways.

The story of the navy crewman's solo air guitar concert had spread fast, gaining extra kudos and growing in audacity with each telling, and his mass 'rendering safe' was already legendary in a war that was only a few weeks old. Rumour spread that the crewman, Chief Petty Officer Gary Brinklow, was leading the scoreboard by a clear mile.

When that rumour reached the SSM, he made it well known that his personal opinion on the theory of troops keeping a score of how many Screechers they had killed was a very poor one, and that if such behaviour were to be taking place, he would happily discuss it with any man in private. When that rumour went around the island, faster than the story of the air-guitarist, mentions of scoreboards vanished instantly.

The island itself was already inhabited, albeit at less than half the population of its usual full capacity, because many people had simply upped and driven away as soon as the news of London's fall had gone public. The occupants, both original and refugee, now faced that difficult transitional period when civilian areas found themselves occupied by troops on active service.

The problems facing any garrisoned troops had only slightly varied since the invention of troops themselves. When you take a trained man full of vigour and tell him that he has to sit still and wait to go to war, then the energy stored in that man leaks out like a compressed gas. Add to this already toxic mix the presence of alcohol and females, and it was like looking down a barrel to see if a gun was loaded. For that reason, Sergeant Swift of the Royal Military Police and his men had been asked to take up one of their original roles and patrol the island in order to ensure no offence was offered to the residents. Johnson, with the approval of Captain Palmer, the necessity of reporting to whom was becoming familiar, had issued the standing order that no man was to consume more than a single pint, lest anyone find themselves unable to defend the population from the enemy through drink. A single pint wouldn't touch the sides of most of the men, but it assured that even the lightest of light-weights wouldn't find themselves incapable of performing their designated role. Each troop sergeant had responsibility for ensuring that he knew where his men were at all times, which made their already difficult lives less enjoyable. The majority of the men had got word to their families when they were first activated, and in addition to the now roughly one hundred and sixty fighting men they now had, they had more than that number in civilians who had either made their way to the camp or had been rescued. The camp, as well-stocked and equipped as it was, was protected only by a tall chain-link fence that Johnson feared could too easily be overrun. That was why he'd ordered the entire squadron and their civilian guests to move for the protected spit of land, and he never second-guessed that decision as the swarm that had come for them would have poured over those fences like water.

Dealing with the internal issues was more complicated than the external. The men with the most engineering knowledge, coupled with a few men living on the island, had been tasked to clean up the hatchet job they had done on the bridge parapet, using the only tool they had at their immediate disposal; the 30mm cannons on their Fox scout vehicles.

Now, using more appropriate tools for the task, the parapets were removed from the first three-quarters of the bridge and work was well underway to build a sloping choke point that could be blocked with the slab-sided back end of one of their Chieftain tanks. One of those tanks, commanded by Captain Palmer, was equipped with the heavy plow blade on the front edge, which was there in anticipation of having to move obstacles to the advance of vehicles, such as crashed cars as well as deliberate barricades. That plow was set to work in a very different way now, scraping the flattened and ruined bodies of so many dead off the roadway. With no way to safely dispose of them, and not wanting to risk burning those bodies for fear of attracting more Screechers, they were pushed into whatever hollow dips of ground could be seen, until earthmoving equipment was brought from nearby. A tired looking JCB, ancient but still as mechanically effective as the day it rolled off the production line with bright yellow paint, made short work of the task, but still, when the wind blew occasionally from the inland direction instead of from the sea, it brought with it a very unwelcome smell of death and decay.

The tank blocking the causeway entrance to the island could be driven forwards and the road opened for vehicles to roll out, but it meant that at least one tank had to remain in situ at all times.

"Can't see that as a problem," Captain Palmer said to Johnson cheerfully, "not much call for heavy armour and the big cannons at the moment, eh?"

"No, Sir," Johnson said woodenly, fearing that he would lose direct control of the next mission, as the Captain would insist on leading from the front if not confined to the slower tank.

"I'm well aware that you are capable of leading the men,

SSM," Palmer said more kindly, as he intuited the reason for Johnson's bland response, "but the higher powers will probably insist that I take the lead whenever we conduct a mission."

Johnson knew he was right, he knew that the joint forces command operating out of a vast warship wouldn't allow a reservist warrant officer to bear the burden of command now that the army had regained a semblance of control over the resources they had managed to cobble together, but it still stung him to have to go back to administrative duties when he had been at the tip of the spear. He had expected to have been pushed even further down the food chain and thought that more helicopters would come to deposit officers to run things, and more regular troops to take control of his squadron.

That didn't happen, and after two days of waiting for orders they were told to wait some more, and grudgingly passed off with the standing order to 'consolidate and resupply at your discretion'.

Captain Palmer, along with Squadron Sergeant Major Johnson, decided that this meant they were to conduct daily patrols, retrieve supplies and ammunition at every opportunity, as well as actively search for survivors.

Which was precisely the reason why they were planning, with the Royal Navy pilots and the Marine Lieutenant and his sergeant, the best way to get troops back to the base they had abandoned and bring back a few Saxon personnel carriers for the Marines to have road transport that was bite-proof.

"Air insertion," said one of the pilots, a man junior to the main 'stick', Lieutenant Commander Barrett, "it's the quickest way."

"It may be the quickest, Lieutenant," said Lieutenant of Marines Chris Lloyd, "but the risk to my marines from the noise that would make is unacceptable."

The two men glared at each other, which Johnson saw, and he sighed internally. If anything, he expected the confrontations to be between his troopers and the Royal Marines. However, apart from the small fracas between two soldiers who should have known better, the main rub was between the three out of four arms of the British military present.

It was the pecking order, as confusing as it was, that was causing the problem.

Marine Lieutenant Lloyd was junior to the Royal Navy Lieutenant James Morris, who in equivalent Marines or Army rank would be a Captain. Captain Palmer found himself technically senior to both co-pilots and all army and marine personnel. However, he was also technically junior to both primary pilots, with their Lieutenant-Commander ranks making them the equivalents of Majors.

Had that rub extended into the non-commissioned ranks, the senior Navy airman would be junior to Johnson, equivalent to his Quartermaster Sergeant Andy Rochefort, but senior to all the troop sergeants and the marines NCO.

When trying to explain, it really messed a person's head up. The simplest way was to assemble the senior officers of all factions and hash out a plan that everyone agreed on. That agreement was proving difficult to find, as the balance of risk was always against the men actually on the ground.

"If I may, gentlemen?" Captain Palmer interjected gently in his velvety voice that seemed to be either a family birthright or a hard-earned skill. His brother had yet to master that skill, as his own attempt sounded infinitely more nasal.

"I agree entirely that any risk to the men on the ground is unacceptable," he paused to smile almost apologetically at his peer, Lieutenant Morris, "so I would suggest a quieter approach. Our aim is to bring men to the camp, secure a few vehicles and return here unmolested." He scanned the room, silently offering anyone a chance to add anything of relevance. "And we agree that large numbers of fighting vehicles attract just as much attention as the aircraft at our disposal. The problem with using the armoured vehicles is that there is insufficient passenger capacity to transport your fellows," he said with an almost regal gesture towards Lieutenant Lloyd, "so I propose that we send a pair of the Bedford trucks loaded with personnel to bring back the things we need. With the Bedfords, we can also take full advantage of being on-site to acquire additional ammunition."

He smiled in a self-effacing manner designed to indicate humility and allow the confidence of his suggestion to be taken without any sense of domineering arrogance. It worked.

"And this additional ammunition?" asked Lieutenant-Commander Murray, "Will two trucks be sufficient to carry everything back? If your chaps are already clear of the area, we can drop in to take another five tonnes if needed."

The implied fact that taking just some of the ammunition would be foolish meant that if they were raiding the ammunition dumps, they would remove the lot. Palmer, appearing for all the world to have not considered what his esteemed colleagues from the Royal Navy's Fleet Air Arm could offer in addition to his plan, beamed at him.

"Outstanding!" he said as he turned to the SSM and addressed him prestigiously in front of the other officers, as his rank allowed, "Mister Johnson, do you foresee any issues with that?"

"Not at all, Sir," he said as he dropped into the rehearsed routine easily and pretended not to have planned for this with Palmer before the meeting, "it would mean a couple of our lot staying on the ground to organise the loading, say four men and two tonnes each? We could get that loaded and be out of there in no time, and there would be no risk to the marines as they'd be safely away by then."

"QMS?" Johnson enquired politely of Andy Rochefort, "did we bring any cargo nets?"

Rochefort frowned and answered that, much to his evident

annoyance, they had not. The easiest way to get a load out via helicopter was to sling it all in the heavy cargo nets the squadron was issued with for exactly that purpose. It was how they had trained for replenishment drops in theatre, but somehow, they had been overlooked. Johnson hardly blamed the squadron quartermaster sergeant for that oversight, especially seeing as the man had located bayonets for their issued weapons, which most of them had never even seen before. The only hassle with slung helicopter loads was the tricky business of having to earth the static electricity so that the unlucky trooper underneath didn't get an extremely uncomfortable jolt.

"We do it the old-fashioned way, then," the SSM said to the room.

It was agreed, set for just before dawn the next day with grid references and radio frequencies agreed, and the conversation turned to more mundane matters. There was to be a small patrol that afternoon to keep up with their daily schedule, and that fell to One Troop, with a single Bedford accompanying their cars to act as an oversized shopping trolley. They still needed building materials for erecting the high fences on any section of the island that could be vulnerable to a corpse or two washing up.

Such needs were recorded, assessed for priority, then set for discussion. When that prioritised list was agreed, the logistics of such matters were worked out and that was where the locals became involved.

Palmer junior, as much as he complained that removing him from the sharp edge of operations maligned his honour, actually enjoyed remaining as the liaison between military and civilian life. He held meetings, fed information back and forward, and when such mission-critical personnel or intelligence arose, then he would ensure that the right connections were made.

For this particular mission, the priority having been made

to secure the island over performing another run for food, he brought forward a young man who worked at a trade builders' yard. He would know precisely where the necessary resources could be found for building the fences, and after that, the troop on the ground would acquire anything that they needed for the defences on the bridge to make them higher and stronger.

That unelected group of civilians which met with Lieutenant Palmer daily comprised four people; three already living on the island and one young woman who had been rescued by their first sortie into the large town. The young woman bore a mottled scar down the left side of her face, which she believed made her ugly and which she tried to hide with her hair falling over her face. She could not, however, disguise her figure, despite the drab green of army uniform that she was still wearing.

————

Some fifteen miles away, the young boy quietly slid the bolt home high on the wooden front door. He could barely reach it on his tiptoes, but he was determined.

He was so determined that the very idea of survival was a foregone conclusion to him; he would not get caught by the things, the zombics, and he would continue to live as he had done for the last few weeks building up to that high bolt that did not want to slide across.

Alone, transient, and quiet.

He had discovered over a fortnight previously that keeping to a conventional and civilised human timetable was not the way forward, as the things were far more active in the daytime than at night. Twice he had almost been caught and had run from a small mob, until he realised that creeping around in the dark was much safer.

It was true that sound seemed to carry further in the dark

dead of night, but he had learned to counter that problem too, and muffled his newly-acquired trainers with large socks to dull the sound they made. He still had his battered camouflaged backpack, only now it had evolved to be stuffed with useful items and he had been forced to carry another bag for new things he had found.

He moved from house to house, often staying still for two daytimes of sleep until he noticed that the occasional straggler had decided to wait outside the house and moan gently. If he revealed himself to it, it would let out that ripping, screeching sound that seemed to tear his insides and he would be forced to run again. He guessed that his smell was attracting them, so instead of staying at a single house to use up all of the resources there, he ate the best of it as soon as he secured the building, then raided the cupboards quietly and methodically, until he felt the need to move on before he became the local attraction.

Another thing Peter had noticed after that first week was that the things were much fewer in number, as though the majority of them in the area who had all flowed through his family farm in a stinking, terrifying tidal wave of noise and teeth, had simply carried onwards to somewhere else.

As much as the memory of barely escaping an awful fate at the hands and mouths of that wave scared him, he tried in vain to figure out where they had been going and, more importantly, if they would be back.

Satisfied that his new home was empty of anything animated, or reanimated, he slipped the straps of his backpack off to rest it on the sofa in the lounge next to the leather-effect satchel he had been carrying in his left hand. The pitchfork occupied the right, and the sanded-down grip of the shotgun protruded out of the top of the backpack, and both of those weapons now rested on the coarse, brown cushions. Peter slipped the belt of ammunition for the shotgun over his shoulder to drop it down next to the bags. He was too slim by far to wear it as a belt and instead it adorned his chest diagonally as a bandolier. He had only used the shotgun once, when he had been forced to be loud in order to prevent a hungry businessman eating him, and its devastating effect gave him confidence, if only to know it was with him.

He wandered the house again, an improvised weapon not unlike a large ice pick still in his pocket next to the folding knife, and he drew all the curtains slowly to settle down for the day's sleep.

THREE

As soon as the single shot echoed between the low hills, and the radio sparked to life, Sergeant Strauss ordered his men to start their engines and proceed. After no more than two hundred metres, two shapes emerged from the foliage at the right side of the road and stood to become the Royal Marine sniper team who had been ahead, and they looked at the target to see if any of the troublesome fast ones were there. The convoy slowed, and the two men, covered in carefully placed grass and twigs to make their suits and helmets blend into whatever surrounds were there, climbed aboard the Bedford truck in the centre of their five-vehicle convoy.

'Limas', they called the faster ones, using the phonetic L for Leaders.

Leaders and Screechers, Strauss thought, *at least it's simpler than Soviets and terrorists.*

Like a lot of the men in the Yeomanry squadron, Harry Strauss had conducted two active tours in Northern Ireland; one as a trooper and one as a Corporal, and the daily fear of not knowing who your enemy was had left him with memories he didn't particularly enjoy. As inhuman as it sounded, he like most of the men, would have preferred a real, traditional war against the armed forces of another country. He wanted to practise his craft without the political worries and fear of prosecution, not out of any bloodlust, but for a desire to prove himself capable in his chosen, if secondary, profession. Now, seeming to get his wish, the enemy was clearly defined. Dead people walking around trying to eat him and his men were quite obviously hostile, and as not one of them had ever registered understanding of a verbal warning, they had free rein in rendering safe the Screechers as and when they had to.

The addition of the marine sniper and his spotter had been at the suggestion of their officer, who seemed almost desperate to get his boys in the war. The capability of that two-man team was an incredible tool, if a little overly precise, and the rendering safe at distance of one of the Leaders was welcomed.

Strauss drove in the lead wagon, his head sticking out of the commander's hatch, but with orders for the driver and others to stay closed down under the safety of their hatches. The risk, he felt, was his to take. Besides, he was controlling a GMPG machine gun with a belt of two hundred rounds ready to let fly, so he felt fairly safe.

Arriving at the builders' yard, he dismounted his and two other of the four-wheeled scout tanks, and they cleared the building as the last armoured scout car stayed closed down to offer the support of the big guns, should it be needed. The Bedford, with the two marines now stripped of the ungainly sniper suits, had also dismounted, and were scanning the area from their kneeling positions at the rear of the truck as they peered down the barrels of their black and green assault rifles and the glinting tips of the fixed bayonets.

"Building is empty," Strauss announced as he returned to the fresh air and slung his sub-machine gun on his back, "let's do this." And with that, three civilians were herded off the back of the truck and everyone but the crew of the last car and the two marines shuffled in and out of the big building, carrying the wooden posts and rolls of heavy barbed wire that would fortify their island even more.

Strauss himself, enjoying the few benefits of rank, didn't engage in the fetch and carry as he maintained overall control of the operation. His own men, the twelve crewmen of his four well-maintained Fox scout cars, all knew him well enough to know that he didn't consider himself so precious as to think manual labour was beneath him, and all of them respected him.

With the exception of one man, but then again Sergeant Strauss believed that he had the measure of trooper Nevin, and knew him to respect nothing; least of all himself. The man's sullen laziness and his characteristic lack of effort offended Strauss because he knew that most of it was an act. Nevin played the fool intentionally, claiming not to understand how things worked so that others would just give up trying to educate him and do it themselves. What annoyed his sergeant so much though, was that he knew the man to be capable. He was a decent driver, never needing to be taught anything twice when it came to something he liked doing, but when the time came to clean down their wagons and gear, or to conduct routine mechanical maintenance, he would find such childish excuses to avoid work that he was universally avoided by most of the men. Socially the story was different, as others liked to be around him when the drinks were flowing, because he was entertainment.

Twice before he had been put on charges for fighting when drunk, not counting the most recent incident that the SSM hadn't fully dealt with yet, and on the last occasion he had been charged by the police for head-butting an off-duty policeman in town. In addition to the fearsome kicking he had received, he faced disciplinary proceedings from the army, pending the outcome of the case, which was likely to result in a fine and compensation.

The case never got heard, in fact it wasn't due to be heard until the week after everything went to shit, Strauss remembered, so yet again trooper bloody Nevin had avoided the consequences of his stupidity. Just as another roll of heavy wire was hauled up and manhandled onto the bed of the truck, his voice cut the air.

"Sarge?" Nevin whined to him, prompting an eye-roll in no less than four of the soldiers, including Strauss.

"What is it, Nevin?" the sergeant answered with a warning tone in his voice.

"I need a shit, Sarge," Nevin answered with a smirk, either ignoring or not recognising the warning. Strauss temporarily lowered his weapon along with his head, which sagged before he drew in a breath, and then he raised his head to fix the smiling man with a look of annoyance.

"Out the back," he said in a voice full of exasperation, "Harris, go with him and make sure he doesn't get lost, will you?"

Trooper Harris nodded, managing to keep the 'why me' from his face, then nodded to Nevin to follow him behind the building, as though he were the unruly child of the troop and it was his turn to reluctantly be in charge of him.

———

Sally Crawford had been a housewife, and she had lived a very happy and satisfied existence until three weeks ago. She had been living in her comfortable semi-detached home, her husband had done well for himself, which had allowed her to have her own car, and that was only a year old. Her husband had gone to work one morning, driving his large Volvo estate that she jokingly referred to as The Hearse, and she had waved him off from the deep bay window in their front room. Turning to her two children, a boy and a girl born only thirteen months apart, she hurried them along to make sure they got to school on time.

Driving her own car, a Ford Orion that she was very proud of, even if the difference between that and her previous Ford Escort was subtle to the point of invisible from some angles, she took them to school and thought nothing of the roads being almost abandoned. She arrived at the school to find the gates closed and a lone teacher outside with a clipboard, who informed her that, unfortunately, the local authority had asked for all schools to close.

She assured Mrs Crawford that nothing was wrong and that it would all blow over soon enough, of that she was sure.

Turning to her children in the back seat, she smiled broadly and told them that they had got an extra day off. She smiled at their excitement and shot the teacher a withering look as she drove away.

Waste of my time, she thought to herself, *they could've at least telephoned me.*

Brushing away the negativity, because that was just the kind of woman she was, Sally smiled and turned up the radio as a Madonna song had started playing that she knew Charlotte, her eldest, liked. She smiled as she drove, stealing glances in the rear-view mirror to see her daughter mouthing the words with intense seriousness as she framed her face with straight hands and struck different poses.

Still wearing the smile reserved for her beautiful children, she hurried them up the stairs to change into other clothes and then spent the rest of the morning making craft projects with them. When midday came, she made herself a modest sandwich and joined them on a rug she had laid out on the lounge carpet so that they could enjoy an indoor picnic.

They went to their own room in the afternoon to play, and

Sally turned on the television. Her face fell as the reports clogged up each channel, telling the horrific tale of the mysterious disease spreading across London and taking with it waves of violence and mayhem.

She shot up out of her chair, flew to the telephone and dialled the agonisingly slow telephone number for her husband's office in the dock almost ten miles away.

It rang and rang, making her knit her brow and replace the handset. Dialling again, frustrated that there were two nines in the number, she listened to the chirping tone indicating that the phone was ringing but nobody was picking up. Replacing the handset to pace again, she cursed under her breath and filled her growing fear and frustration with being busy.

She cleaned her kitchen, then tried the number again. No answer.

She scoured the Littlewoods catalogue until she found the replacement home telephone she would ask her husband ever so nicely for. She would tell him how tiresome it was to call him at work with that silly old dial phone, and then fix him with her best look, where her eyelashes fluttered ever so slightly, and he would see that as some indication of nuptial promise.

She could get anything out of him when he got that look in his eye, and all the nice things in her home were the result of individual manipulations.

Just as her stress and worry started to become the first inklings of panic, a screech of tyres and a crash sounded from outside. Running out of the front door, she saw her husband's Volvo parked at an angle on the driveway and her own car shunted diagonally as he had hit the front wing. Gasping loudly, as much for the new car as at the fate of her husband, Sally ran to him and saw instantly that something was wrong.

He was sweating profusely, his loosened tie and unfastened collar soaked through below his bright red face. He was gasping for breath, his eyes rolling, and she leaned in just as he let out a croaking noise that sounded like he was winded. He shuddered once, made another croaking noise and went still.

Sally screamed his name, pulling open the door and trying in vain to pull him from the car by the hand. She screamed and dropped his hand, seeing that the very tip of his left little finger was missing. The stump ended in a red wound, already dry and scabbed over, and she held her breath to force herself to retain some control before she became useless. She stepped forward again, calling his name loudly and slapping his cheek lightly with her right hand. That hand suddenly stopped moving as he lifted his head again, turned his face and locked his teeth onto her wrist. He bit down hard, breaking the skin and cracking something within the joint to make Sally shriek in agony as she threw her body weight backwards. Landing heavily with her left hand wrapped tightly around her injured right, she looked at her husband with shock, because he had turned to face her and was reaching with both hands, moaning and making a gargling, hissing noise at her.

His eyes were cloudy, his mouth hung open and blood mixed with spittle as it ran from the lower corner of his open maw. Sally rose quickly to her feet, fearing that her husband would attack her again, but her stressed brain finally acknowledged that her husband was still secured inside the car by his seatbelt.

Leaving him where he was, she stumbled back through the open front door and ran her bitten wrist under the cold tap in the kitchen. To her surprise, the wound had already stopped bleeding but felt swollen and hot to the touch. She staggered into the front room, feeling lightheaded, and began to dial the three digits to call for the police, but the length of time it took the dial to return to zero saw her faint to the carpet after the second nine.

Sally's children had been singing along to the tape deck in Charlotte's room, and were unaware of the slight commotion downstairs, so they had no warning when their mother opened her milky eyes and followed the sound upstairs to where they played in blissful ignorance.

Later, after she had gorged herself, Sally wandered back down the stairs with the front of her pretty dress sheeted in blood. She walked aimlessly out of the front door, pausing only briefly to look at the thing struggling weakly in the driver's seat of a Volvo, and walked off, dismissing it as inedible.

————

"Just hurry up so we can get back," trooper Harris said to Nevin, who was dragging out the task so as to avoid any form of hardship. Nevin chuckled from behind the tree he was using as cover for his squat and made intentionally foul noises with his mouth to annoy Harris.

It worked, as Harris tutted and walked a few paces further away from him.

In the small patch of woodland behind the builders' yard, a woman in a dirty floral dress with one shoulder pad torn and hanging down her right arm, turned her head slowly towards the sounds. The blood that had covered her front had been washed away by rain, and further degraded by her walking around for three weeks to provide the result of the dress being torn in places that could excite a soldier.

That was, if she didn't have the clouded-over eyes and pale, mottled grey complexion of a Screecher.

Turning her body to point in the same direction as her face, she emitted a low, gargling hiss and set off towards the source of the noise. When she reached them, she heard two people talking. She didn't know they were people and her destroyed brain had no way of interpreting the noises as defined speech, without the higher functions she had once possessed. She had no cognitive ability, but she was attracted to the sound and the closer she got to the sound the more she could detect movement. With that movement came the smell of the living, and with that smell came an apparent aggression and lust for warm flesh that spurred her instinctively onwards.

"Oh-Jesus-fuck!" Nevin blurted out as he almost fell backwards with unfastened trousers in a desperate bid to locate his personal weapon.

"Oh, don't be a fucking idiot, Nevin," Harris snapped at him, finally breaking and deciding to let the troublesome soldier have both barrels. "You just can't help yourself being a twat, can you? Every fucking time there's work to do, you find some excuse to piss about and… *aargh!* You *wanker!*"

Nevin made desperate noises and pointed behind Harris, who was so annoyed with the man's stupidity that he ran out of words, dismissed him with a wave of his hand and a noise of disgust and turned away.

Directly into the path of what used to be Sally Crawford.

———

"Last one?" asked the tall man, who had evidently worked at the yard, as he indicated that the room in the truck was all but taken up. Strauss nodded in agreement, then froze as the scream of a grown man in agony ripped the air in two.

The two marines had already set off for the rear of the building at a dead run, followed by Strauss and three others.

Rounding the edge of the building, he swore loudly as he heard the sound of automatic gunfire erupt.

"Hold! Hold!" he screamed, both in frustration at the person firing and at the marines ahead of him, as he had seen the rounds hitting the damp earth ahead of them. The marines had seen it too and threw themselves against the corner of the brick building.

"Hold your fire," Strauss bellowed, hoping for a response

from the person behind the weapon. From the noise, he knew it to be the same Sterling as the one in his hand, but then again, both men he had sent back there were similarly armed. The firing stopped, although more likely caused by an empty magazine than by common sense regaining control, and Strauss took his chance to break cover as he told the others to stay where they were.

He rounded the corner just in time to see Nevin slotting a fresh magazine into the side of his weapon, complete the reload and raise it to his shoulder. Ignoring the risk of a ricochet hitting him, Strauss ran hard at an angle for the rest of the scene to emerge.

He saw Nevin leaning into his weapon as he fired more careful, measured shots. He saw Harris, at least he assumed it was Harris, lying flat on his back and twitching his right boot like a tap dancer. He saw a woman, her modesty unpreserved thanks to the holes torn in her dress and saw fresh blood on her as well as the stains of old blood. He had seen enough people like that over the last month; normal people lifted from their everyday lives and cursed to wander the earth in a ceaseless search for food. This woman had been pretty. Had obviously cared about her body and her appearance. Now she was riddled with bullets, staggering back upright to her feet and tearing the air in between the gunshots with that awful screeching noise.

Nevin, a third of the way into his second magazine, had still not brought her down. Strauss knew the man, knew that he scored acceptable scores on the range days to qualify on the weapon in his hands, but could only attribute the appalling inaccuracy to fear and panic.

Fear and panic were the weapons of their enemy, and his trooper was more danger to himself and his own side than to the lone, unarmed female Screecher in front of them.

"Cease fire!" he bawled angrily, not caring about the noise, seeing as the automatic fire had likely already attracted every Screecher in the area to their location. Nevin stopped, shaking and wide-eyed as he spun towards Strauss and forgetting the basics of weapon discipline. Inadvertently pointing the barrel of a live weapon at his sergeant's chest, Nevin watched as the gun was slapped away from his grip.

"Safety that weapon, Trooper," Strauss spat at him, then took two swift steps forward to spear Sally Crawford upwards through her open mouth and stop her shrieking for good. He didn't spare her a glance as she fell to slump down, because he was already turning to the reliable man from another crew in his troop.

"Harris? Harris?" he said insistently, "can you hear me?"

The moaning and twitching man moved his hand away from his face reluctantly before clapping it back to the wound and keening more loudly, hearing the sergeant's response.

"Oh fuck," Strauss said, before turning and shouting for a med kit. The marine spotter arrived first, slapping a heavy gauze pad onto the ragged patch where Harris' right cheek used to be.

"You'll be alright, son," he said to the stricken man as the rest of the troopers picked him up bodily to take him back to the vehicles. Strauss picked up Harris' gun, checked to find that it had not been fired, and looked at the Screecher for the first time since he had rendered her safe. He slowly broke his gaze away and looked at Nevin, then back at the woman. Turning back to Nevin again, he inclined his head to indicate for him to move ahead of him. That look alone promised that the matter was far from over.

FOUR

"Sir, patrol reporting that they are on the way back," Daniels told Johnson, wearing a look that indicated clearly there was still bad news to come.

"And?" the SSM asked.

"And they are reporting a casualty. One of our troopers has been…"

"Bitten?" Johnson asked in a quiet voice to break the painful silence.

"Yes."

Johnson took a sharp breath in through his nose before blowing it steadily out of his nose. He asked for an estimated time of their arrival and left.

Finding his only superior, ignoring the junior officer who was, in his opinion, a very well-polished turd in a tailored uniform, he cleared his throat to interrupt the conversation Captain Palmer was having with Lieutenant Lloyd of the marines.

"SSM," he acknowledged, reading his facial expression perfectly, 'do we need to speak privately?"

"In front of Mister Lloyd is fine by me, Sir," he said with a nod to the Lieutenant. Johnson liked marine officers, as they endured the same hardships as their men and as such, formed a tighter bond with them, he felt. Army officers were sent to what he considered to be the most expensive boarding school going, only to learn to act as though the men under their command were the scum of the earth. No matter how badly they treated the scum, they still fought like the devils and drilled like guardsmen in the desperate attempt to gain their superiors' acceptance.

"One Troop is inbound, but they have a casualty," he told them. Palmer's face screwed up in sympathy briefly, and he asked who it was in a concerned voice.

"One of the troopers, Sir," Johnson told him, suspecting that he might have seen a small drop in the man's shoulder signifying relief. If he had read that right, he could only assume that it was relief that the injury wasn't to a civilian.

"It's the nature of the injury that's the cause of concern," Johnson explained, "it's a bite."

The two officers looked instantly drawn.

"Is he running a fever yet?" asked Lieutenant Lloyd.

"No details as yet," Johnson answered, "but they will be here in minutes."

"The man needs to be quarantined, Sergeant Major," Lloyd insisted, "One of our chaps was bitten at Heron," he explained, using the Navy's own name for their air squadron at Yeovilton, "and he ran a fever until he died, then he…" Lloyd paused, then seemed to decide that he had no better way of explaining it, "then he came back and turned on his mates."

"Timeframe?" Palmer asked.

"From bite to turning? Within the hour," was all that Lloyd could say.

"If you'll allow me?" Johnson asked politely, meaning that he wanted the captain's leave to issue orders ready for the arrival of the returning troop. Palmer nodded and followed him.

"Daniels? Get the tank moved and rouse the standby troop. I want them at the foot of the bridge now."

Daniels nodded and began to give orders into the array of radio sets in front of him, not that Johnson saw, as he was already heading down the slope at a jog to be at the roadway before the others.

The standby troop the forces kept at the ready to respond to anything, was Sergeant Maxwell's assault troop. He gave Maxwell a short version of events and explained what he needed from him, then turned away as Maxwell gave his own order for two men at each end of his long line spread out across the road, who promptly disappeared to bring what they were ordered to. The noise of engines grew until the returning troop rolled in, stopping when instructed before reaching the island itself.

The hatch of the lead vehicle, Strauss', was up and he held a hand to his ear to hear the questions shouted by the SSM.

"In the Bedford," he yelled back, pointing behind him unnecessarily.

The armoured cars were waved through and instructed to park. Only Strauss was permitted to leave his wagon, and the others were ordered to shut down their engines but stay where they were.

The terrified civilians were first off the truck, their eyes wide and their breathing fast. They were the ones who had been on the island when it had all started, so they hadn't experienced the fear of coming close to the Screechers before. Johnson climbed up to see a trooper he couldn't recognise due to the blood and heavy dressing on his face. The man was strapped down, and it took him a moment to recognise that he was secured around the torso, his arms pinned to his sides, with heavy-duty grey tape.

Johnson looked to Strauss, who seemed to understand the question.

"Couldn't run the risk of him turning and being able to move," he explained simply. Johnson looked at the man's feet, seeing that his knees and ankles were similarly bound.

"Trooper?" he asked, giving the man a fairly robust poke in the shoulder.

"It's John Harris," Strauss said, earning a grunt from the SSM.

"What happened?"

"Two of the lads were out back behind the target building, a Screecher attacked and bit Harris," he reported bluntly. What he didn't say gave more indications to Johnson that what he did.

"And our other man?"

"Nevin," Strauss answered simply, making Johnson suppress a growl.

"Get him inside," the SSM ordered, then stepped back to allow the flurry of movement his instructions had sparked. He saw the two marines, the sniper and his spotter, talking quietly to their Lieutenant, who looked up to meet Johnson's eyes before an apologetic look washed over him. Johnson decided to ask the direct question and walked towards them.

The marines stepped politely aside, allowing the SSM room.

"Anything I haven't been told yet?" he asked curtly.

The Lieutenant looked to his sniper, then back at Johnson before instructing them.

"Tell him."

"Sarn't Major," the sniper said politely, "not my place to say, but your man, Nevin?"

"What of him?" Johnson asked, barely keeping the contempt at even hearing the man's name from his words.

"He froze. Emptied an entire magazine at the thing and

failed to bring it down. He was fucking about, begging your pardon, before that and was trying to shirk the hard graft," the marine said without emotion.

Johnson couldn't be sure what annoyed the marine most, the unprofessionalism of the man or the unforgivable inaccuracy of his shooting. Johnson himself could forgive neither.

"Thank you," he said, "I trust you'll keep this to yourself?"

The three marines nodded, and Johnson glanced to the Lieutenant to be sure he got the message.

"Get yourselves squared away then," he instructed his two men, leaving him alone with the SSM.

"This is an isolated matter, Sir," Johnson told him formally, "one bad apple in my whole squadron, and he won't be an issue again."

"I understand, Sarn't Major," Lieutenant Lloyd said in an equally formal tone, "but I'm sure you will also understand that I may be forced to insist on my marines being present for future missions. We are after all the specialist infantry."

Johnson had to agree that the man had a point. As proud of his soldiers as he was, the majority at least, they were still reservist cavalrymen and could not expect to measure up under intense pressure against the Royal Marines Commandos.

"Lieutenant," he said seriously, "I may just insist on that myself, so long as we can get your boys appropriate mounts in the morning."

"Make way," Johnson boomed as he scattered the rubbernecking troopers out of the way, "anyone not directly needed here is to piss off to your duty stations. Now!" he added unnecessarily, as the soldiers had already begun to crowd at the door like rats escaping when the barn lights came on.

He found Harris in a bad way, with the marine's own medic attending to him, seemingly voluntarily.

"Fever's already got him, Sir," the marine said, his

Midlands accent alien to the south coast, and his eyes conveying more than the words meant.

"Get him comfortable, if you can," he said, then watched as the man administered two syrettes of morphine directly into Harris' thigh. The breathing rate stayed high, but the rasping sounds that came from the unconscious man's throat lessened. They watched as the breathing continued to grow steadily slower, then Harris' open eyes widened with each gasped breath inwards. As the breathing stopped, the tension in his body lessened and the heat seemed to bleed away from him.

Johnson placed a hand to Harris' face, reaching out to close his eyes when the marine snapped a warning.

"Don't!" he said as he got to his feet and stepped away. "Help me," he said, then he pulled a strip of the same tape used to secure the body and began to strap his chest down to the table Harris lay on. Passing it under the table as they wrapped it round, ducking and rising with each turn, they both leapt back in unison as the last time they stood, they were being watched. Harris' eyes, turning in an instant from the dead eyes of a human to the milky orbs of a Screecher, were fixed on Johnson. The trooper drew breath in to prepare a shriek of excitement and frustration at being denied his meal but stopped short as the marine swore loudly. Harris snapped his head towards the man, fixing him like a computer-aided targeting system, and drew breath in again.

He didn't get chance to issue the shrieking noise, as Johnson's bayonet punched through his right temple and into his brain. Having to use his left hand to hold the flopping skull still the SSM withdrew the blade with great difficulty.

Training note, he told himself, *aim for the eye socket unless you want to lose your bayonet.*

Silence hung heavy in the room as both living soldiers looked at the twice-dead corpse in disbelief.

"That was fast," Johnson said, seeing the man opposite him

nodding but keeping his eyes on the body, "Was it that fast with your man?"

"What?" the marine said in confusion, "Oh, not sure. It wasn't our man, it was on the other side of the airbase."

"So…" Johnson said, trying to frame the question correctly to get the information, "were you told that your marine *turned* that quickly?" he asked, wincing at the terminology he had just used.

"They didn't say," he mumbled, "but did you see how quickly he changed?"

"I did," Johnson said, then turned to leave the room, "can you please put my trooper in a bag and we can organise a proper burial?"

———

"Good God, man. You're proposing that we order our men to kill one another at the first sign of injury?" Captain Palmer asked incredulously. The man was so well-bred, so exquisitely mannered that for him to show such emotion betrayed how truly shocked he was at the suggestion.

"If it's from a bite, Sir, then yes, but only a bite," Johnson responded flatly. He stood stock still, semi-rigid as though prepared to stand to attention if not most of the way there already. He fixed his eyes on the corner of the ugly picture frame on the wall behind the captain and stared straight through it.

"I can't issue that order, SSM," he replied, "it's barbaric. It's inhumane, it's…" he paused, unable to locate the words he wanted to best describe how he felt about the suggestion, "… it's just not the way we do things, man!"

"I appreciate that, Sir," Johnson said patiently, "but the fact remains that we are outside the normal parameters of war. This isn't the fight we've been trained for."

Palmer sat down in a chair and crossed one leg over the other. In other men the gesture would appear almost feminine, but something about the way he did it made it stylish. Johnson sat down next to him, explaining again how rapidly Harris turned. He described the burning hot fever, how he had been incapacitated almost as soon as the bite occurred, and how once his breathing had stopped, he was ready to tear chunks out of him inside of a minute.

"Sir, if we allow injured men back inside the wire, we will be done for," he said calmly, "I started a procedure today that we need to stick to whenever anyone goes off the island. The returning men have to strip down and be inspected to be sure that nobody is hiding a bite and thinking that they'll get better. They have to have their temperature taken for signs of fever and anyone displaying signs we aren't happy with goes into a holding area. That's the only way we can be sure not to bring back the disease, and yes, it may be barbaric but by God it is necessary, Sir."

"Quite right, Sarn't Major," he said, using the enlisted men's vernacular for his rank, as he often did without making it sound unnatural, coming from him, "I trust you'll make the necessary arrangements whilst I pass this on to our naval colleagues?"

"Consider it done, Sir," Johnson replied, because him asking permission from the captain was a formality.

He had given the orders twenty minutes prior to the meeting.

———

"On your feet, *'teeenShun*," Strauss barked, seeing Nevin fly up to his full height and stamp to attention as Johnson walked in the room. Nevin's face registered many things; guilt, dread, remorse as well as fear that the Sergeant Major would hit him again.

"Thank you, Harry," he said, not taking his eyes off the trooper before him.

"Sir," sergeant Strauss answered, then left the room. Nevin's eyes flickered towards the doorway, knowing that the last witness had just left him alone.

"What am I to do with you, Nevin?" Johnson asked in a low voice, receiving no answer.

"It occurs to me that you might be fucking up intentionally to try and avoid work," he said as he took a step back and looked down on the man, "which I thought was the reason for your stunt in the Royal," he mused out loud, meaning the Royal Arms where the fight had broken out, "Do you want to get locked up, Nevin? Do you want to get your arm broken so you don't have to go out there and you can stay here, where it's safe and no nasty Screechers want to bite your face off?"

At the mention of biting faces, Nevin quailed and Johnson knew he had broken the façade.

"Tell me what happened to Harris," he ordered him in the same measured voice, "and in case you're thinking about leaving any details out, I already know. I just want to hear it from you."

That bluff, a common one with senior NCOs, was one that no solider in their right mind would bet against. Men at that level seemed to have eyes in the back of their head, in addition to their ability to read minds and hear the faintest of whispers clearly over long distances.

"I told Sergeant Strauss I needed a shit, Sir. He instructed Harris to go with me and I stalled for time to avoid the work detail," he admitted in clear, confident sentences, "One of them came out of the woods and I tried to warn him. He didn't believe me. It bit him, and I fired on it, but the fire was ineffective."

Johnson stepped closer again to interrupt him. Everything Nevin had said rang true with the story Strauss had told him.

"So you avoided work, put another trooper in danger to cover your charade, then you were too much of a clown to warn the man that he was in said danger, and *then*," he snarled, "then you panicked like a child and wasted ammunition until your sergeant had to save you. Tell me if I'm wrong?"

"No, Sir," Nevin said flatly.

"No, Sir," Johnson mocked him, as though Nevin had woken up and decided to play the soldier a little too late, "You've got a man killed, put a dozen others in jeopardy, shamed your unit and embarrassed us all in front of the regulars, the navy and the marines. You are a fucking liability."

"Yes, Sir," Nevin said, his voice cracking.

"Christ, man... a child is more worth to my squadron than you are."

FIVE

Peter always wanted to be a soldier. He knew that he had to wait for his sixteenth birthday and that his parents had to sign a letter giving him permission to do so, effectively handing their child over to the army.

Peter was fine with that, and he doubted if his parents would have missed him if, well if they had both still been alive.

That was his plan to escape, to get away from them and the life he had endured, and it was nothing to do with seeing the world or learning a useful trade; it was just a means of escape.

In many ways, the sudden change in his existence of having to hide from people who wanted to hurt him meant little variation to him, but instead of the abusive parents he'd had to contend with, he had to try not to get eaten. He kept to his new routine of resting up in the daytime and moving every second or third night, sometimes only half a mile and other times much, much further as the distances between villages could be vast for short legs.

This decision to become partly nocturnal, like all the adaptations to his new life, was less of a cognitive process and more of a feeling that he acted upon. He probably couldn't have articulated these decisions very well, but they had kept him safe and, more importantly, thriving. On one of the days when the sunlight was dancing off the tiny particles of dust floating in the air as the beam of yellow light streamed through the gap in the thin curtains he had drawn, noises brought him out of the sleep he had been in. He shuffled over to the edge of the mattress, crossing the distance on the soft double bed he was treating himself to sleeping in, and swung his legs down. Slipping his feet into the new trainers he had found in a previous house, he stepped lightly to the window and knelt down so that he wasn't obviously visible, should anyone glance up at him.

He told himself *anyone* instead of *anything* because, as far as he knew, the zombies didn't drive cars.

Peeking through the gap at the side of the curtains so that he didn't move them, he watched as a dirty, dull blue coloured car drove up. It was about the same size as the one his parents had and it rocked slightly as it was stopped by the handbrake. The engine was off, and a man climbed out from behind the wheel to look around in all directions. He had a beard that didn't seem right, didn't seem deliberate somehow, like it didn't suit him, and wide eyes in the gap between that beard and the unruly haystack of hair on top of his head. Those eyes scanned up and down the sparsely populated street they were on and evidently assured him that they were alone, because he reached back inside the car and took out a long crowbar, which he took with him to a house. He used it to stab into the wood near the lock of the door, then he turned back over his shoulder, calling out to the car and gesturing with his head. The sound of the car door opening drifted up to Peter, hidden by the small tree that obscured the rest of the vehicle from his view, and another man walked reluctantly over to join the first man, with his shoulders sagging, as though being forced out of the seat had annoyed him. He put his body next to the bearded man and they leaned their combined weight against the long edge of the metal bar, making the sounds of cracking and splintering wood echo up to the young boy watching them in secret. He watched them go into the house, heard the distant, muffled sounds of glass breaking, then it was his turn for his eyes to grow wide as a scream ripped out of the open door three times louder than the sound of the smashed glass.

Peter stayed glued to the show, unable to move and freezing in some form of self-preservation response, and he watched in horror as the bearded man reappeared at the front door, dragging something behind him. The burden must have been heavy, because the thing he was dragging seemed to be dragging him back.

Then it screamed again, spun around, revealing shoulder-length dark blonde hair plastered to its face, and began to hit at the hand locked onto the collar of her jacket. The other man, younger and smaller but now far more alert than he had been going in, enthusiastically followed her out and offered encouragement by way of light kicks to her legs and backside. She screamed and struggled, trying to get back inside the house at any cost.

Peter's eyes narrowed, and his heart grew cold.

It was fifty-fifty which house he had decided on that morning, choosing the one he was in because the moonlight had shone on it and it gave him a better view through the downstairs windows. He felt a mix of relief that they weren't taking him, and guilt that he had chosen differently and someone else was suffering. And she was suffering. The man with the beard hit her, hard, two or three times before dragging her up and forcing her into the car. The door was shut on her, leaving her lying flat on the back seat as the screaming and struggling stopped. Peter thought that they must have hurt her badly or knocked her out, then gasped and moved back involuntarily from the window as he saw both men looking in his direction. Inching back towards the window, he looked down in horror as one of the men went out of sight under the mantle of the front door.

Just as the thud of metal on wood echoed up the stairs.

Peter rose to his feet carefully, his unfastened trainers slipping slightly as he reached for his jumper and bags. He never went to sleep undressed, not fully anyway, and his bags were never left in an unpacked state. He made for the doorway, stopping to look at the dark space under the bed and dismissing it instantly as too obvious. He knew, again not that he could articulate it, that getting downstairs and out via the back door was an impossibility as the sounds from the ground floor of the door breaking were already loud. Instead he turned, looked at the three doors in the upstairs landing, and selected the one that he knew would be the airing cupboard.

Opening it, he placed his two bags on the lower shelf and slipped the sawn-off shotgun out of the top of his backpack. Climbing into the first partition, the one just below eye height, he rolled over the stack of folded sheets to a space behind them and pulled the door as far to being closed as he could from inside, where there was no handle. He clutched the handle of the shotgun, with the shortened pitchfork pressing uncomfortably into his back as he couldn't bring it to bear in the cramped confines of the cupboard. The shelf above him blacked out the light as it was full of stacked towels, and he pulled a light pink sheet over him to complete the transformation. He drew in a breath, held it to absorb the smell of clean laundry, then let it out slowly just as the front door splintered inwards.

Muffled sounds from downstairs made him think about the layout. The heavy, thudding sounds of boots moving over the wooden floors in the hallway and lounge. The almost sticky sounds of the soles of those boots on kitchen linoleum, then the near-silent footfalls betrayed by creaking steps as those boots came up to his level. He shifted the grip on the shotgun, the cold metal of the shortened barrels feeling slippery in his warm hand, and he concentrated on keeping himself still and quiet.

A loud crash indicated the boot forcing its way into the bathroom. The sound of the cupboard being opened and slammed back closed painted a picture in Peter's mind, and the footsteps going soft again told him that the search was continuing into the room he had just vacated. He closed his eyes, recalling the picture his mind had taken when he left and assuring himself that he had left no sign that anyone was there now. He heard the footsteps pause, heard the sound of the curtains being snatched open and then drawers being opened and closed roughly.

The sound of a car horn from outside made Peter jump, biting his lip to keep quiet, as the man searching the house snarled just past the partly open door.

"Fucking idiot," he muttered.

Peter held his breath, willing the swearing owner of the heavy boots to go back downstairs. Agonising seconds ticked by before he did, letting Peter allow himself precious seconds to breathe and slow his heaving chest. He listened to more shouts outside, unable to make out the words, but highly attuned as a natural empath to the moods of others, to know that the voice was angry. The car started, a belt in the engine shrieked in protest, and the sounds of the engine died away.

Peter relaxed. That was a bizarre side-effect of his low standard of life before this happened; he could correctly recognise and detect a person's mood in seconds, often without them even saying anything. It was how he survived his family. How he knew when to make himself scarce to avoid becoming the focus of unwanted attention.

He climbed carefully out of the airing cupboard, gathered

his belongings and crept down the stairs to peer into the sunlight to make sure that both men had left in the car. He felt bad for the woman, but some part of him was grateful that it was her and not him, as his young brain didn't fully comprehend why she would be valuable to the men. He tightened the straps on his bag and looked up and down both sides of the road, expecting at least one of the things to have come to investigate the noises they had made. He saw none, but he knew that didn't mean they weren't coming. Just as he went to walk in the direction they hadn't driven off in, a noise from the house opposite caught his attention.

Stepping closer so that the roof line of the house blocked the sun that shone directly in his face, his eyes fixed on the source of the noise.

Standing just beyond the broken front door, eyes rubbed red and nose streaming, was a girl who couldn't have been more than four years old.

———

Johnson used a commandeered car to visit the three sections of sandy beach on their tiny rock that had been deemed vulnerable to a sea-borne attack. Perhaps attack wasn't the right word, but the little patches of smooth approach from the water were vulnerable if they considered how many Screechers might be milling about in the low tide and likely to wash up there by random chance. He watched the tall fence posts being driven deep into the sand and the wire being strung between the posts. Walking up to one strand snaking diagonally across the height of his chest, he reached out to twang the cord of viciously barbed, twisted metal and felt it give a few inches. Opening his mouth to ask why the wire was neither straight nor strung tightly, he closed it again.

The design was intended to keep an unthinking human

body wrapped up until such time as a man with a fixed bayonet could render it safe.

He completed his rounds, finding the materials in place for the other defences, but the work not yet underway. He was pleased to see that three men were at the beaches, alert and confident. Being in a civilian vehicle allowed Johnson to drive past slowly and not interfere, and it also allowed the men to pretend that they hadn't seen their commander and continue their vigil. He found the troop sergeants, giving them the written orders to reinforce the difficult words he said.

"Jesus," cursed the commander of the assault troop, Maxwell, "really?"

"Afraid so, Maxwell," Johnson answered solemnly, "anyone outside the wire from now on has to go to into quarantine for three hours, which we think is more than enough time to be sure there aren't any infections."

Maxwell nodded his understanding, with his discomfort evident on his face.

"I need you fit for the morning, Simon," Johnson told him in a tone of voice that conveyed his confidence in the sergeant and his men. "I need two wagons from your troop to run the operation."

"Just two?" Maxwell asked him with a furrowed brow.

"Yes, two Spartans and two Bedfords with the marines. Your men can help get a few Saracens up and running, hit the ammo dump, then everyone moves out."

"Everyone?" Maxwell asked, letting Johnson know that some communication between army and navy clearly existed.

"Apart from a few who will be waiting for the helicopters to load another few tonnes of kit," Johnson confirmed.

"But you want the armour gone by that time, obviously?" Maxwell asked him, not imagining that his commander would risk having vehicles in the open with the sound of two helicopters attracting every Screecher inside a wide area directly onto them.

"Indeed I do," Johnson answered, "five a.m., if you please," he finished, giving the time as a statement and not a question. Maxwell nodded, and the two men broke away.

Johnson spoke with the officer commanding the marines, reiterated the plan, then checked the troop guarding the causeway and turned in for the night.

Because he had won the argument to lead the mission leaving in the dark pre-dawn.

———

Peter froze, almost unable to comprehend what his eyes were seeing. The child was no longer crying, but simply staring at him and giving an occasional spasm of inward breath with a trembling lower lip, as her dark golden hair was stuck to one side of her face. The startling similarity between her and the woman he had seen being dragged away made it clear to him that there was an obvious family connection.

Peter turned away, hearing a gasp and a small sob, so he turned back and took a step towards her, which made her whimper and take an involuntary step backwards. The sporadic gasps of inward breath that made her small chin convulse had slowed now, but her red-rimmed eyes still stayed locked on Peter, despite their puffy appearance. Slowly, Peter crouched to put down the pitchfork and bag, then slipped one arm out of the straps of his backpack and swung the bag to his front, all the while keeping his eyes on the girl in case she bolted. Reaching carefully inside, he found the thing he wanted near to the top and pulled it out.

Holding out the sagging, tired-looking stuffed lamb towards her, he gave it a small shake as though trying to entice her with it. Its limp limbs wobbled comically when he shook it, and she rewarded him with a tiny giggle and took a hesitant half-step towards him. The two, both on the same eye level as Peter was still crouching down, were separated by only ten feet of open air and the threshold of the broken house when another noise sounded.

It tore the air, making both of them jump as the hissing, screeching shriek struck fear into him and sheer terror into the girl. He snatched up his things as he moved forwards seeing her shrink away but not run; evidently her mind recognised that some things were more frightening than others. Peter thrust the lamb into her arms as he threw the bag back around onto his back, then readied his pitchfork after pushing the door closed without being able to shut it.

Nothing happened. Behind him the girl stiff sniffed and sobbed very softly but did not cry out loud; probably a reaction she had been forced to learn quickly or she wouldn't have survived that long.

When Peter could no longer stand the tension, he rose slightly and handed the girl the other bag he couldn't carry if he wanted to use both hands on the weapon, and he nodded to reassure her as she took it awkwardly. He ushered her towards the nearest door and tried to get her inside, but she shook her head and her chin began to tremble once more. Peter knelt before her, telling her in a tiny whisper that it was okay and that he wouldn't hurt her and that she should stay inside and be very quiet. He told himself he was saying anything just to get her to hide in silence, but when he promised her he wouldn't leave her, something hardened in his heart and he realised in that tiny, split-second moment that he meant those words.

The shriek sounded again, closer this time and from just the other side of the shattered door frame. Peter pushed the girl backwards and closed the door in her face to plunge her into the darkness of the pantry cupboard, then stepped quickly to the side of the entrance that led directly into the kitchen. The door pushed open, tentatively at first, then harder as the thing outside must have smelled them. It stepped inside and swept its head to the right just as the fingers of Peter's left hand found something behind him on the wall.

On instinct, snatching up the small bunch of keys from the hook, he tossed them out ahead of him and watched as the thing took two fast, staggering paces towards the sound the keys made as they hit the wooden floor.

Then he struck.

Taking his own strides into the fight, he thrust upwards just as the thing turned. Both spikes of his pitchfork had been aimed to penetrate vertically into the skull of the monster via the neck, but the speed with which it turned threw off his aim and resulted in the prongs coming out of the face without damaging the brain. The hideous image this gave took away his courage momentarily, but at least the injury he had inflicted served to keep the beast's maw firmly closed as it tried to close its fingers on him. Taking his right hand off the shaft of the pitch fork he reached for the single spike, once a piece cut off the tool which he now carried as a weapon, and he twirled it in his fingers to reach upwards and spear the stinking thing in its left eye.

The struggle ended instantly, with the zombie sinking to the ground as he withdrew both weapons. Only then did he see the monster as the person it used to be. A young woman, younger than the one he had seen dragged not long before from the very house he was in now. She was wearing the light blue tunic of a nurse and she had the curious look of half a perm, as the left side of her hair was matted to her skull with dried blood. He read the badge on her chest, Joanne, and the logo of a care home for the elderly he had seen when he had first walked into the village a few days before.

A creaking noise made him ready the weapon again and

bare his teeth in natural response to a physical threat, and he dropped both instantly when he saw the little girl had pushed open the door of the cupboard he had put her in.

Stepping around the kitchen counter that luckily blocked her view of the dead thing, he took her hand and led her out of the back door.

SIX

A clear thirty minutes before the four a.m. wake up in readiness for the start time of their five a.m. mission, Dean Johnson had already risen, shaved in a small sink of cold water, dressed for combat and was finishing his second cup of coffee.

That was his normal morning routine; get up, drink coffee, go about his business and drink another coffee. On the days when he really meant it, he could get himself squared away so efficiently that he could pour both drinks from the same kettle and drink them both hot. He was not a man, as he put it, to fuck about. When there was work to do, he always had the mindset of getting it done as quickly and efficiently as possible, then when there was nothing left to do, finding something worthwhile until the end of the day.

In his civilian life, that of being a skilled mechanic working on the larger engines of heavy haulage trucks, he was so far ahead of his peers because by the time they rolled into work, he had already done three hours' worth and had broken the back of the day's tasks before his first break. In stark contrast to his military career, this hard work left him working on the shop floor and not scaling the ladder to management, simply because he was too damned valuable where he was. That wasn't to say they didn't pay him well, and most of what he learned was useful in his military time, as the armoured vehicles of the British army weren't especially known for their reliability.

Now, seemingly wearing his SSM persona in a permanent way, he opened his mouth wider to take in the very end of his coffee, which he drank in the NATO-standard *milk & two*, just as he took his tea, and he made the same mistake that everyone did in their life at some point and underestimated how much liquid was left. Putting the cup down with his cheeks inflated like a greedy hamster, his eyes widened as he forced down the large swallow and coughed slightly.

The small billet he had been allocated was a thin but tall town house near to the causeway entrance and the small square that housed the official pub of the military personnel, as well as the hall that was used as their mixed-forces headquarters. Being the only three senior NCOs, he, Rochefort and the naval Chief Petty Officer were allocated a room each. The houses next door had been offered as more spacious accommodation to the officers, which Johnson was glad that he didn't have to endure, as no doubt they would turn it into an officers' mess at some point and try to out-brag each other with their exploits.

The exception to both rules lay with the Royal Marines, as both their officer and their sergeant insisted on billeting with the men, crammed into three houses in the next street. The island was inhabited to about a third of its usual population, the other portion having upped and left to God only knew where when the fur began to fly. The remaining people, about four hundred of them, had welcomed the soldiers cautiously but had treated the refugees they had brought with them like honoured guests and integrated them quickly to replace the families who were not expected to return. The refugees numbered close to a hundred family, friends and other survivors who the soldiers had found along the way. Now there was the better part of a thousand people living on an island that easily catered for almost three thousand. Given that the single causeway road bridge in and out now had no parapets protecting it from the short drop into the swirling current and was blocked by a Chieftain tank, the human traffic of regular movement had all but stopped.

Johnson knew that the food and supplies issue would raise its head again soon, likely that afternoon. But that morning was about sustenance to feed something more important than the now-unemployed civilian population. Today was about finding bullets to feed their machine guns.

In their few skirmishes prior to the battle of the bridge, they had expended phenomenal amounts of ammunition to counter the massing hordes of stumbling corpses, and they were down to enough rounds per wagon to barely equip them for another defence. They had expended a fair amount of the larger 30mm rounds for the cannons on the Foxes, but 7.62 was the magic number. They had twelve Fox cars, four of the quick and light tracked Spartans in Maxwell's assault troop, as well as the two larger versions of those tracked vehicles in the two command Sultans. Each of those eighteen vehicles had a big, reliable GPMG machine gun, and that was before the two Chieftain tanks counted their two per wagon. On top of that, the SLRs of the small Royal Military Police and the new SA80 rifles of the Royal Marines took different ammunition again. The men of the Yeomanry squadron were relatively well-off for the 9mm rounds to feed their personal weapons but seeing as their specialist form of fighting didn't primarily involve being outside of their armour too much, that wasn't a priority.

Their stockpile, however, still needed doubling to be on the safe side.

There were also rations, fuel, tools, spare parts all to be considered and that was where he had managed to force his way onto the mission.

Captain Palmer, as capable and quick-witted as he was in contrast to his obnoxious and spoilt younger brother, saw the benefit in Johnson's claim and also knew with utter certainty that he had been played like a fiddle.

"It's not a matter of seniority in command, Sir," Johnson told him in a placatory voice, "it's simply that I know instantly what the parts for the vehicles are and how many of what we need."

"And," Palmer said as he completed the thought out loud, "we can't very well both of us go as we would be leaving the remaining soldiers without army leadership. God forbid our chaps should come under navy control."

So it was agreed. Palmer would stay and 'quarterback' the whole mission via the command headquarters. His choice of words made Johnson frown as he thought of how to phrase the question. Palmer saw the look and told him anyway.

"My first posting in Germany," he said, "was with an American unit as liaison. I spent more time in an Abrams than I did in a Chieftain for a little under a year before my chaps deployed for a large training exercise and I got to go back. Some things one just, sort of… absorbs, if you follow my meaning?"

Johnson did, and if he was honest with himself, he was a little jealous. Shaking that away, he tried not to smile too much at having shoe-horned himself into a key position before the bureaucracy of the military served up another plate of humble pie for him to eat and forced him back down the chain of command even further.

He was surprised that hadn't happened already, as there was obviously an element of command and control still in play and apparently, floating at sea, was a growing fleet of allied nations becoming involved. He was certain that, after the arrival of the navy and marines bearing the knowledge that senior commanders were still in charge, they would send a Major at least or a Colonel to take over command of the army's resources on land.

That hadn't happened, and over the coming days it was clear that their little green slice of southern England was relatively unimportant to the bigger picture, where the disease had already spread over Ireland and mainland Britain. There were pockets of survivors here and there, according to the eyes very high up in the skies, but anything resembling a large town or city was destroyed. The main concern, Johnson had soon realised, was the spread over continental Europe.

He was entirely ignorant of the 'how' part, and he doubted that if anyone floating out in the Channel knew, they would bother to tell a reservist Warrant Officer, but the disease which was believed to have originated in London had found its way to a Paris outskirt within a day. His mind ran riot, thinking that it could only be that someone who was infected had got onto a boat or passenger ferry, and been inadvertently taken to France, where they had started biting people like there was no tomorrow.

That was how the British Army of the Rhine was so heavily engaged, and why the thought of their return to British shores to eradicate the outbreak there was an impossibility.

They were, for the most part, on their own.

What he didn't know and could probably have worked out for himself, had he been in a sufficiently dark mood as to contemplate such things, was what was happening in the wider world.

The United States, as was sensible, had ceased all movement into the mainland. Traffic in and out of Canada was allowed, but their southern borders were closed by a massive mobilisation of the National Guard, and their seaward borders were patrolled day and night by the combined might of the navy and coastguard. There was a widespread decree from their president that there was 'no way on God's green earth' that disease would enter their land. There was widespread outcry for the US to bring her troops home to fight the good fight, but on that subject the president was ominously silent.

The south American continent, much in the same way, mirrored those actions. As did Australia and many African provinces, and Japan, along with any island nation in possession of their own naval forces or under the protection of another country.

What was most worrying, however, was the posturing of the Soviet Union.

––––––

"Morning, chaps," Johnson said in a low voice out of respect for the ungodly hour. The assembled marines, almost all of them, he guessed, were clustered together near the two Bedford trucks parked ready the previous night to carry them to the camp. The same camp that the army had sensibly abandoned, before the tide of dead had swelled to a size that would have washed over those thin fences and swept them away.

He received the expected grunts in response, some calling him 'Sir' and others using his rank but none of them offering any disrespect. The smell of hexi-blocks, the solid fuel used to heat water in their mess tins, mixed with a waft of cigarette smoke as he passed the men. Maxwell was ready, using the wagon that he had fixed in record time under interesting circumstances during their recent battle. He'd had to repair the gearbox linkage before their tenuous position had come under friendly fire and forced them to abandon the vehicle and give themselves yet another obstacle to overcome. He had made the repair, incredibly, and had limped home to regain the safety of the island just before the horde had reached them.

The reason Johnson had chosen Maxwell, other than the fact that he was a capable leader of troops, was that he commanded the faster tracked vehicles and the other sergeant he trusted had lost a man the day before. Putting the remaining men of One Troop straight into another mission was out of the question, and Johnson had to admit to himself that although the men of the other two troops were effective at performing their conventional roles, he didn't think they had fully switched on to their new reality. Leaving those men as steady guards of their island and confident that they could serve their guns effectively should the need arise, he elected to take the men most accustomed to dismounted reconnaissance.

Half of his assault troop were in their two chosen Spartans, with another four of them designated for the front seats of the Bedford trucks that would transport the Marines. Johnson climbed aboard the front Bedford's cabin, relegating his trooper to the breezy canvas-backed rear section, and he opened the window to rest the barrel of his Sterling sub-machine gun on the ledge. The driver, the round-faced and smiling trooper Povey, was rolling a cigarette when Johnson climbed up, and he turned to see Povey offering the little cylinder to him. Johnson didn't smoke as a habit, but he was known to feel the urge from time to time.

"Thanks," he said, reaching out and taking the smoke, allowing the trooper to light it before leaning back to watch him roll a replacement with deft fingers. The men knew that the time for hot drinks and cigarettes would end soon, as they would be observing 'hard routine', just as they would in any danger area, because they couldn't run the risk of attracting the Screechers through something as unnecessary as tea or a smoke.

Just as the sun began to rise, Captain Palmer stepped out of the headquarters building and raised a tin mug in salute to the big man riding shotgun in the big, green truck as they set off gently down the slope.

SEVEN

The phone rang, shattering the underground silence and echoing terribly. The man in the white coat ran for it, snatching up the handset and hunching down as he cradled it with both hands for the precious promise of life that it could bring.

"Hello? Hello?" he hissed into it desperately, hoping that he hadn't imagined it again and that there was actually someone there this time.

"Professor Grewal?" enquired an efficient and polite female voice from the other end.

"Yes," he croaked, then cleared his throat, "yes, I'm Professor Grewal, who is calling?" he asked, wincing as he heard the mania in his voice but was powerless to prevent it escaping.

"Hold, please," was all he heard, then a click on the line and he was certain that he'd imagined it. He flopped backwards against the wall next to the phone and slid down to sit on his heels. If he wasn't rationing his food to the point that he was borderline hypoglycaemic constantly, he might have had the tears to spare but as it was, his body would not part with anything it could still use. He sobbed with dry eyes as he suffered another minor panic attack, reliving the terrifying events of the last three weeks spent underground.

He had been mostly underground for a few months before it all went wrong, but before his experiments for the government, the government of which country he couldn't be entirely sure, went wrong and released hell on earth, he had at least been free to leave.

He had no clue how severe the outbreak had been, but he knew enough to realise that nobody had come to rescue him yet, so that meant things obviously weren't going too well topside.

He was a leading expert on biological outbreaks, with a background in applied chemistry, which had allowed him to create and test the perfect pathogen to destabilise a foreign country. That knowledge sadly offered him little solace now, not knowing what was happening outside of his underground lab, which he had managed to secure by some small miracle.

By combining a particularly aggressive strain of rabies courtesy of the Americans, with his own modified version of meningitis, he had created the perfect antidote to humanity, and had inadvertently unleashed a plague destined to make his own species consume itself into oblivion.

The outbreak caused by the human testing phase of his work had at least been contained in the lab, but the protocols had sorely overlooked the unexpected side effects, and the team sent in to help those trapped inside were the ones who released the infected into the streets of south London on a Friday afternoon.

Grewal had been trapped inside a small storeroom with no water and had suffered for two days until he finally steeled himself to make a desperate bid for freedom, or at least another room that had food and water. He had found rolls of insulating wrap in that storeroom and had wound it around himself as a crude form of bite protection in readiness for his escape attempt.

Events above ground, as devastating as they were to the entire south east and spreading west with enough raw power to halt an armoured column heading to restore order to the capital, had actually saved him from death by dehydration or worse. When the gathering mob above ground began to move with some bizarre, unknown singular purpose and started to march together, the two lurching former colleagues who were camped outside the door to his storeroom were distracted by the sound they were all making, and stumbled their way towards the exit to join the exodus.

Feeling desperate, he psyched himself up to fight his way out, only for that desperation to turn to foolishness as he shouted a short squawk of challenge to the empty corridor. Realising that his besiegers had gone, he forced the main door closed and locked it, returning to the carnage that used to be his state-of-the-art lab. There were parts of bodies strewn over the floors, which he tried not to look at, but the most worrying discovery was the test subjects still strapped to their gurneys.

Some had tipped themselves over in their thrashing attempts to reach flesh with their teeth and Grewal watched in horror as they seemed to emerge from a state of dormancy when he walked in the room. Their cloudy eyes fixed on him and any noise he made fired them up until they began to shriek and hiss and snap their teeth together in his direction, as though they could bite their way to him despite being restrained.

As traumatised as he was, he was still a scientist who felt not only personally responsible for the catastrophe but believed he could fix it.

He first looked at the only test subjects to be still and saw a pair of surgical clamps buried through the right eye socket of one. Another appeared normal to look at, but closer inspection revealed the hilt of a scalpel protruding from the base of the skull.

Over the next few days he took samples from them after doubling the restraints and being very careful to never make contact with them without protective gear. He collected the samples and his test results, then dispatched all of the still living men.

Not *living*, living, he supposed but at least still moving.

"Professor?" asked a voice from the phone, startling him back to the present.

"I'm here," he said, "who is this?"

"Commander Briggs of Her Majesty's Royal Navy," came the insistent response, "Professor I can't be certain that this form of communication will last long so I need you to answer my questions as efficiently as possible. Do you understand?"

"Yes," Grewal stammered.

"Are you injured or infected?"

"No."

"Is the lab still secure, is it accessible from the outside?"

"Yes," Grewal said, then thought before answering the second part, "and I'd need to open it from inside."

"Do you have hazardous material from the lab and is it secure?"

"Yes, in a hard case. I have blood and tissue samples and…"

"Please," Briggs interrupted in an admonishing tone, "brevity and accuracy are key here, Professor. Do you have supplies to last for a month or more?"

"No."

"Do you have supplies to last *up to* a month?"

"No."

"Dammit," Briggs said cursing him pointlessly, "can you hold out for a fortnight?"

Grewal did the mental calculations again, having emptied

every piece of edible material in the lab onto the large table in the common area.

"Eleven days, maximum," he said weakly, hearing breathing and a pause on the other end of the line.

"We will attempt an extraction as soon as possible," Briggs told him, "We will attempt to use this method of communication to warn you closer to the time, but it may not be possible. Be ready."

The phone clicked again, and the line went dead.

"Please," Grewal said in a small voice, "don't leave me alone... talk to me, please..."

He dropped the phone and sat with his back to the wall as the swinging handset bumped off his shoulder with a pendulum motion. Just then, whether from sadness, desperate loneliness or relief, the tears came and would not stop.

EIGHT

"Thank you, Private," said Kimberley Perkins to the soldier flanking sergeant Croft with a cup of tea.

"No, Miss," he said looking confused, "I'm a Trooper, not a Private."

"Oh," she exclaimed, as she looked up from the strong-smelling tea cupped in both hands, "sorry, I er… what's the difference, if you don't mind me asking?"

Trooper Cooper, as much as he had heard of the jokes about his name and rank, didn't mind at all. He glanced at sergeant Croft, seemingly to ask for permission to engage in idle chitchat with the civilians, and he received a nod of consent. Cooper sat next to the young woman, seeing her shrink slightly away and self-consciously fuss with the hair on the left side of her face to hide the bumpy skin of the scar.

"We are a squadron, see, made up of troops of troopers, but the infantry has regiments made up of companies of privates. There are some gunners and fusiliers and scaleys bu…" Croft cleared his throat loudly without looking up from his clipboard, and Cooper amended his explanation, "I mean signalmen," he said sheepishly, "so it depends on where you get put in the army."

"Oh," Kimberley said again as she looked up into his kind face, "so the men with the red berets and different guns are privates?"

"No, Miss!" Cooper chuckled, "they're all…" he paused to look at Croft's back and evidently decided against using the nickname he had loaded ready to fire, "they are Royal Military Policemen, RMPs, and they come out of the factory as Lance-Jacks, so they can order people around, like," he said, unaware that his explanation raised more questions than it answered.

"Lance-Jacks?" she asked, confused.

"Yeah, half-screws? One-stripers? Lance Corporals. 'Cept their sergeant, who is a sergeant, obviously," he responded.

"Lay off, Cooper," Croft said tiredly, "can't you see you're confusing the lady?"

"It's fine, Sergeant," Kimberley said with a smile, "bullshit does baffle brains, after all."

Croft gave her a warm smile, guessing incorrectly that she had heard the terminology from one the men in his squadron.

"But I'm not bull…"

"Thank you, Cooper," Croft interrupted quickly, "off you go now."

Cooper rose, looking slightly hurt, but Kimberley treated him to a kind smile from the visible side of her face, and that pleased him. As he left, Quartermaster Sergeant Rochefort walked in and sat down with a nod to Kimberley.

"Tea, Andy?" Croft said.

"Yes, please, Tom," he replied tiredly, then rubbed his face.

Kimberley smiled again. She loved to watch people interact, especially soldiers, and saw no bigger change in them than when their subordinates left them in peace and they could revert to their peer group settings. The exception to this, she found, was the officers, who seemed to retain the same lofty sense of superiority regardless.

Seeing the two tall, confident men relax made her feel more at ease, and she almost let out a small titter of laughter when the two men moaned and groaned at their aching joints as they sat down.

"Miss Perkins," Andy Rochefort said, "how are you on this fine, if not rather early morning?"

"I'm well, thank you, Staff," she answered, betraying that she had been doing her own research other than to ask Cooper.

"Andy, please," he said with a smile.

"Very well then, but you can call me Kimberley, just not Kim," she said in a voice than invited no disobedience or further inquiry.

"Understood, loud and clear," he answered, "now, I also understand there are some concerns from the people?"

"Yes, well, not so much concerns as needs really," she said, fidgeting with her hair again and automatically turning her face so that she spoke to them sideways, "the supplies from the shop are all gone, as you know, and there are people, ladies specifically, who need certain things…"

"Ah," Rochefort said, intuiting the subject she was trying to raise without needing her to use the words. The dead giveaway for this was the sudden absence of the men appointed to the task of ensuring effective two-way communication, "say no more. I presume you have a list available of the items?"

Kimberley did, and she gratefully handed over the folded piece of paper from the sheaf in front of her.

"There are other pressing matters," she went on, "other than the island-wide shortage of toilet paper."

The three of them chuckled politely at the small joke, allowing other matters to be brought up. Kimberley enquired politely about the soldiers who had left that morning, asking when they might be back, just as a rushing, intense noise filled the air above the building they were in, and blasted away with a dizzying Doppler effect which was repeated seconds later.

"That would be their taxi going to collect them now," Croft said with a smile as Kimberley tried to figure out the logistical sense in what he said.

———

The gates of the camp came into sight of Maxwell's wagon at the head of the convoy of four. The two vulnerable trucks were in the middle, with the other tracked vehicle at the rear. They moved fast, keeping a good distance in between their vehicles, and only stopped when they reached the gates.

More than a few Screechers had wandered out in the road after they had passed, and two had even stepped out in front of them to be crushed under the tracks of the lead wagon. Johnson, from his elevated position in the first truck offering a good view ahead, guessed that these were two of the Leader types of Screecher, the ones the marines had been calling Limas.

Faster and more capable they might have been, but they couldn't evade ten tonnes travelling at over fifty-five miles per hour.

Maxwell dismounted with the other trooper from his wagon, leaving the driver in place, and pulled the gates open to allow the four vehicles inside. There was a fleeting urge in Johnson's mind that they should cowboy it; that they should just bust through the gates like in a film. He brushed that thought away almost immediately as stupidity. He would never destroy a perfectly good barricade which could be used against the enemy.

They closed the gates afterwards, jogged back to their mount and drove on. The camp was a big place, and when they had resided there briefly, they'd only used a portion of it and kept the fences clear. They had to push much further in to achieve their objective this time, and the mood in each vehicle felt tauter and more expectant with every inch they travelled. The enormous hangars filled with vehicles, found easily as the man driving the lead wagon had been there many times, was opened to reveal the rows of angular, brutish lumps on their four massive wheels.

The marines had all dismounted when they stopped, pouring from the back of the trucks to the rhythmic noise of boots hitting the tarmac, to take up defensive positions, as the others sorted out the selection and starting of four Saxon armoured personnel carriers. The four men assigned to drive were all from the Yeomanry, seeing as armoured vehicles were primarily their arena, even though none of them had ever driven them. They were deep inside the complex layers of fenced sections, so highly unlikely to encounter any enemy, but that didn't prevent the marines from demonstrating their field-craft, which seemed to come as naturally to them as breathing. Johnson paused a moment to take in the sight of them, either lying flat or kneeling to cover every square inch of approach through the sights of their new weapons with the alien appearance of the magazine being housed behind the trigger grip.

The marines were very different from the men of Johnson's squadron, and as their new trucks rolled out, they climbed aboard via the double doors at the rear. Two trucks came under the direct command of their officer, and the other two of the sergeant who had been introduced to Johnson as Bill Hampton. He was at ease with his men, never seeming to feel the need to issue orders, but simply stating what he needed them to do, and they did it. Their current drills were nothing new, as they'd become accustomed to that kind of transport in Northern Ireland, albeit in the previous generation of armoured car.

The two men, Lieutenant Lloyd and Sergeant Hampton,

nodded to one another and the sergeant climbed aboard to lead his two trucks away. This was part of the plan, sending back half of their commandos as soon as they were mobile, and the second half remained with the two tanks and Bedfords. They opened another massive building attached to the workshops and took box after box of vehicle spare parts to ensure their armour stayed mobile.

"Right," Johnson said happily after loading one truck, "bullets."

The ammo dump, stored well away from the buildings and people in either dead or living form, was a few miles from the base. It took them a long time to get through the many physical layers, then the hard work began as they carried large crates out to the one now empty big, green Bedford truck. One squad of marines knelt in cover to point their weapons towards the gate as the truck was loaded up, then yet more boxes of large bullets were carried out to the open square nearby.

"What's their ETA?" Maxwell asked, more out of conversation than needing the information repeated for him. In response, Johnson did that strange thing that people do when asked any question relating to time, especially when it doesn't directly involve knowing what the precise time is, and he glanced unnecessarily at his watch.

"Sixteen minutes," Johnson told him, realising what the question was designed for. Maxwell was offering his opinion that they would have carried enough to fill the helicopters by the time they arrived, so long as they left the island very soon.

"Call them in," he told the sergeant.

They carried the rest, fulfilling the weight quota with rapidly calculated mental arithmetic, and everyone but Johnson and a pair of Royal Marines remounted their respective vehicles in anticipation of the instruction to move.

Johnson glanced at his watch again, seeing that the sixteen-minute window had just expired, and craned his neck to look up as he shielded his eyes from the indirect sunlight. The characteristic sound of helicopters flying, that booming chatter of rotary blades cutting the air, came to him. He turned to the vehicles, raised the thumb of his left hand, and watched as they drove away. Right on cue, the pair of helicopters dropped in, turned and flared noisily to land close to where he stood. He knelt down, screwing up his eyes to save the rotor wash from blowing too much dust into them. Ordinarily, the two Sea Kings would keep their engines turning, but they were adopting new tactics to keep their profiles low in the new war they were fighting.

The first one was loaded, and the aircrew were strapping down the boxes before the blades had even stopped turning. The second one was similarly loaded, and Johnson allowed himself to sink into a narrow canvas chair in the first bird, feeling the ache in his hands and arms and the burn in his shoulders.

As the engines burst back to life and whined up to screaming pitch, he leaned back and smiled at the easy success of the last six hours.

And he prayed it would last.

———

The helicopters landed first, but only by a margin of a few minutes as they had taken a route straight out to sea, heading south before looping a long westerly arc well out of sight of land, to swing back and find the island to their north. That way was intended to avoid the numerous Screechers, who would have seen and heard the aircraft, and followed them back to the island to hold some grotesque reunion of the last time.

The first two Saxons growled their way over the bridge with their dark green and black camouflage seeming just as brutal and inappropriate to the picturesque seaside setting as the tank blocking the roadway did. They followed the new standing orders and went into the buildings to strip down and show the RMPs that they weren't bitten. When they'd been through the initial check, they went into a quarantine building, equipped with tea, coffee and food, where they waited to prove that they weren't running a temperature.

Twenty-four minutes later the other Saxons came back, nestled fore and aft of the heavily loaded Bedford trucks and a Spartan at each end of that convoy, and those men parked their wagons to go through the same process.

Seven hours from start to finish, and they had recovered four new APCs, which would allow the marines to safely conduct their own operations, as well as thousands of rounds of ammunition for their guns. Johnson looked down the slope and smiled as the convoy snaked its way slowly through the obstruction of the tank and the sloping obstacles.

That smile faded as he saw the man climbing out of the top hatch on the Chieftain tank, jumping up and down and waving his arms desperately.

"Stop the convoy," he said out loud, his voice desperate and cracking with the opening stages of panic, but there was nobody there who could turn those words into an order and pass it down to the men in the distance.

He didn't yet know what was wrong, but he was certain that it was nothing he wanted to see up close. He felt worse seeing it from a distance, as he was powerless to stop it.

————

The man chosen to command the second of Maxwell's wagons was Corporal Graham Ashdown. The fact that Maxwell had chosen him spoke sufficiently of his competency, and in fact his hard work saw him on a waiting list for an NCO leadership course, in preparation for him receiving another stripe on his arm.

If anything, Ashdown was a little disappointed in the ease of their mission. Not from any immaturity or lust for violence, but from the point of view of a professional who wanted to showcase his ability to command his fighting unit. Their unhindered route to the camp showed only the rear view of a Bedford truck and the faces of the alert but inert Royal Marines inside as they scanned for threats using the minimal amount of effort in order to conserve their energy.

That was something he found amusing; his own men were known for eating and sleeping at random times, but the marines took it to a new level entirely. If they were stood down for even five minutes, one of them would fall asleep instantly, only to come awake just as rapidly when the order to move came. It was the same with food; when the marines saw it, they devoured it as thought they were rescue dogs living in constant fear of starvation.

He expected at least some employment when they arrived at the camp, but they found it devoid of life, or whatever the state of the Screechers should be called. He had heard the radio traffic about the few who had staggered into the road in answer to the noise of their four loud engines, but most of them faded away into the distance behind them, as only the quicker ones had made it out in front. He saw the evidence of those where they had been mashed into the road surface and flattened in intricate patterns by the tracks of Maxwell's wagon and the two sets of big tyres following, so his only view of the enemy was either squashed or out of range.

The work inside the camp was back-breaking and strenuous but it was good to feel employed, if only for a short time. The Saxons were found and started with ease, and the remaining half of the marines stayed to help load the trucks.

As soon as the helicopters could be heard swooping in,

Maxwell mounted his lead wagon and called the off, leaving Ashdown to take up his position at the rear once more as his convoy of four made their return journey in much slower time, given the tonnes of ammunition and weaponry they had recovered.

"Contact left!" Ashdown called out over the radio, making every head in the convoy snap to their nearside as a dozen Screechers leaked from the close tree line and directly into their vehicles. No gunfire sounded as the distance was too short and the warning too late to bring their heavy machine guns to bear on the ambush, so they relied on their momentum and weight to carry them on through the attack.

Being the last vehicle some short distance back from the others, Ashdown was the first to see it, as he had the best perspective. That said, he still didn't have time to bring the cupola around to fire on the attack, not that he definitely would have, given that there were only a few of them.

The first Screecher to stumble from the undergrowth was unable to gauge the speed and distance of the first light tank as it passed him by, followed by the two big, green trucks. His scarlet-red beret had long since been lost, but the camouflage smock and trousers remained intact, even if the ragged hole in his throat had soaked the uniform almost black down his front.

The last tank, the one his head was turned away from, hit him hard with the very centre of its front edge, which threw him down hard to the concrete before rolling over his thighs with the left-side tracks. Hands reaching instinctively, the Screecher clawed at the smooth underside of the Spartan as it rolled him over and over, dislocating joints and snapping off fingers.

The damage to the once-human body was unimaginable, but it didn't prevent the half-ruined fingers of the left hand gaining purchase and swinging the ruined body around to drag behind the vehicle. The right-hand finger and thumb, all that remained, found a tenuous handhold on the rear and the torso raised itself an inch higher, just as the legs from just below the pelvis fell away to slip from the gory trouser legs and bounce to a gentle stop in the centre of the road.

"Road clear," Ashdown said, making the milky eyes of the hitchhiker snap forwards to seek the source of the sound that its brain associated with fresh meat.

NINE

When she came to, Ellie Finn first opened her eyes and instantly regretted it. The pain in her head was incredible in the most literal sense of the word, and it simultaneously threatened to make her vomit and fall off the hard ground she was lying on as the world spun viciously. She had been unaware of the car journey, but her brain peeked through the fog and she knew that she was in a different place from before the men had broken down the door.

The door. The house.

She sat up, fast and uncontrolled to be hit with another barrage of agony that shot down her spine to the tips of her big toes.

"Amber!" she sobbed, earning another jolt of pain as the words bounced back to her ears and sounded like someone else's. She threw up, hard and uncontrolled, to cover her left leg as she instinctively turned away. Collapsing back and banging her head again she sobbed out loud, repeating the name of her daughter, who had been left behind when the men had taken her.

"Shhh, it's okay," said a voice from behind her in an attempt to soothe her pain.

"It's not okay," she sobbed wretchedly, "my baby," then lapsed back into unconsciousness.

Misunderstanding, the woman who soothed the girl shushed her again and stroked her matted blonde hair. She had lost people, too but had not been forced to suffer the death of a child, as she had none. She could only begin to imagine the pain and loss that the girl was feeling, even before the men who had 'saved' the crying, wounded woman had roughly dumped her unconscious into the same room as her.

It was a cell, regardless of what they called it. Any room that someone else forced you into and locked the door on was a cell, whether it was built for that purpose or not. The younger woman had been there for a day and a night, after her own little corner of quiet safety had been invaded by the sound of a shrieking fan belt, and her front door had imploded. The men she'd met had invited her to come with them and seeing no choice but to comply or get herself hurt, she'd gone with them. She wished she'd had the strength to overpower them, but she highly doubted she could have incapacitated two of them with a swift knee to the groin before one of them had used the weapons they carried to hurt or threaten her. Meekly, she had gone with them and she'd regretted that decision every minute of every day since.

Now, seeing a younger girl dumped roughly in the room with her, she tended to her as well as she could and waited for her to come around once again.

She awoke an hour later much in the same way. Her hands twitched, and her body jerked as though her consciousness was trapped inside a plastic bag and she fought to punch her way out. When she did, she came awake with an exaggerated gasp and sat bolt upright, only to whine pitifully and sink back down, holding her neck with both hands at the base of her skull. She opened her eyes in response to the voice, unthreatening as it was obviously female, which was trying to calm her again. She cautiously opened one eye, hating the light streaming through the window for burning her retina with its unkind brightness, to see a woman with lighter blonde hair than her own and maybe ten years older. She smiled kindly, weakly as though she was apologising for what had happened to her.

"Careful," she said as Ellie tried to sit up, "go slow, you've got a nasty lump on your head."

She went slowly, raising a hand to her head and the main source of her pain to find what felt like an egg protruding from just behind her right ear. Her stomach went into spasm again, making the other woman step smartly back and snatch up a metal rubbish bin to catch the remaining bile collected in her stomach. Her brain somehow knew that she had already thrown up, but her eyes couldn't find it.

Perhaps she cleaned it up, Ellie thought randomly, just as the jumble of feelings and sensations bubbled to the surface and her heart broke for the third time that day.

"My baby," she sobbed again, screwing her face up and falling back into despair and tears to complement the agony inside her skull.

The woman soothed her again, trying to find the words to comfort her.

"I know, my lovely," she said with genuine sadness for the girl's loss, "we've all lost people to them but I ca…"

"She's not lost," interrupted the girl with slurred words, "she's alive. They took me away and…" she broke down again and her sobs intensified, "they left her there. She's all alone…"

Try as she did, Ellie couldn't help but break down with her and the two women cried together. Resting the girl down on the bed, she stood and began to hammer on the wooden door for attention.

"What do you want?" came an angry response from outside the closed door.

"This woman had a baby with her," she snapped angrily, "where is she?"

A muttered conversation took place on the other side of the locked door, prompting Ellie to bang again.

"She didn't," came the answer, "she was on her own."

"No, she bloody well wasn't," Ellie snapped back, creating more silence and insistent muttering from beyond.

"Okay," said a different voice tentatively, "we'll go back."

––––––

The house was much the same as they had left it three hours previously, only this time it had attracted two of the slow-moving ones who were milling about aimlessly inside the low stone wall of the front garden. The crowbar put an end to one as the other was enticed towards the younger man, who had crudely taped a straight-bladed carving knife to a broom handle. The knife punctured the face dead centre, travelling slightly upwards through the sinus cavity to pierce the brain, and the thing's lights went out.

Both men had enjoyed the killings, but both had distinctly not enjoyed the roasting they had received from Michaels; the man who had bestowed on them the responsibility of going back to find the girl they had apparently left behind through incompetence.

They searched the house again, finding it precisely how they had left it, with just one exception.

The addition of another dead body laid out flat like a starfish on the kitchen floor.

"I didn't do that," said Ian from behind his rough beard to the younger and far less intelligent Carl. Michaels called them Thing One and Thing Two, which Ian had explained to Carl had originated from a children's book. But they still used their real names, despite others mimicking their frightening leader.

"Who did then?" Carl asked, frightened.

"Don't bloody know, do I?" Ian snarled back at him, "But it's a good bet whoever it was took the baby we're supposed to be looking for, so start searching, idiot."

Carl searched, as did Ian. They found nothing else amiss, other than the body with its punctured brain and ruined left eyeball. The back door had been ajar when they'd entered, and that was closed to keep the bad things out, but the destroyed front door would not close. Their arrival had prompted yet more interest, and they were forced to flee back to the safety of their hilltop refuge to report the news of their failure.

––––––––

Peter was forced to change his usual nocturnal routine after the interruption of the bearded man and his crowbar. The shock of finding the little girl still hadn't faded, and their awkward flight over fields from the back of the house was far more diffi-cult than it should have been, because the girl's legs were much shorter than his own. If he'd been a grown up, he would have simply scooped her up in his arms and carried her. He was sure it had been Leonardo who'd scooped April up like that in a TV programme he'd very occasionally managed to see if his mother was comatose. He loved the Ninja Turtles, when he got away with watching it. The one time he tried picking this girl up like that, she'd whined and squirmed out of his grip to shoot him a look of sheer grumpiness. He got the message: don't touch me.

In addition to trying to get her to move more quickly without being allowed to physically help her, he also faced the frustrating limitation of only having one-way communication with her and trying to translate her suspicious looks to gauge whether his words had been understood.

As much as this slow progress frustrated him, the very thought of leaving her to herself was an impossibility. Already in his head, he'd worked out how much extra food and water he would need to carry to keep her healthy, and that was before he even found out if she liked the same things he did; whether she would eat cold beans or rice pudding from the tin. Finally reaching the summit of a low hill behind the village, he paused at the top to assess which direction they should take. Opting for the snaking path that led into another cluster of buildings about the same size as the one they had just escaped, he turned to encourage the girl, who had taken the opportunity to sit down.

Her legs must have been aching, he realised. As small as the hill was to him, it must have been a huge effort for such a young person. He glanced back down the hill, satisfied that nothing was following them, and sat down next to her. Digging in his back pack as she played with the floppy limbs of the cuddly lamb, Peter brought out chocolate covered biscuits taken from the house he'd been in. They'd fallen down behind some items in a cupboard, which he wouldn't have noticed had he not been standing on a chair, and he unwrapped one to see if she noticed. He glanced at her as he chewed the first mouthful of raisins, biscuit and chocolate, to see her eyes watching the treat in his hand intently.

Hungry or not, he doubted he would turn down the snack at any age, so he was sure he had her attention. Holding the other one out to her, he watched as hesitant fingers whipped out to take it carefully, then began to remove the purple paper sleeve and attack the foil wrapper underneath. She glanced at Peter again, just to be sure it wasn't a trick, and bit into it. She chewed fast, not waiting to finish one mouthful before she took another bite, and she finished it before Peter had eaten the last piece of his own. She handed him back the wrapper with a small smile and looked at him expectantly.

"You still hungry?" he asked her. Her wide eyes and blank face showed nothing, but her head nodded twice.

"Let's get down there and find somewhere safe first," he told her in the slightly patronising tone of a young child talking to an even younger one, "and then we can eat, okay?"

She seemed to think about it for a moment, her lips pursing and her fair eyebrows almost meeting in the middle, then she nodded again abruptly.

"What's your name?" Peter asked her, pushing the envelope of their communication to see if she would make words yet, "How old are you?"

She ignored him, rising to her feet and walking away down the hill. Peter shrugged his way back into his back pack, hefted the pitchfork and the other bag, and followed her direction to catch up with her easily. He fell in step alongside her, keeping an easy pace due to the height difference, and told her about his life. He explained that his sister was taken away, and after that all the bad things that had happened. He skipped the details of killing his own mother after the horrendous things he had seen her do, and of the massive riot of dead things who'd walked straight through his farm and made him hide in shit until they wandered off, and about the one he had decapitated with his father's shotgun, after he had cut off the barrels that were too long for him to manage. He kept to the facts appropriate for a child, forgetting to view himself as one, given his experiences, and the little girl listened without answering.

That conversation, such as it was, led them to the hedge separating the rolling landscape from the village. Peter stepped in front of the girl and held a finger to his lips, then handed her the bag in his hand and pointed for her to stay where she was. She took the bag, kept her lips firmly pressed together, and nodded. Peter hefted his pitchfork and crept towards the style, where he could easily cross the wooden fence and step onto the grass verge before the road. He watched, and he listened, hearing and seeing nothing but sure of the knowledge that the absence of those things did not mean for one single second that there was nothing out there, or that they were safe.

Keeping his eyes on the road and buildings, he reached down with his right hand and scuffed about in the earth of the hedgerow beside him, coming up with a small rock. He weighed it subconsciously in his hand, not for a precise weight but for an instinctive feel for the effort it would take to launch the missile, then heaved it up and over the hedge to make it skitter along the road where it bounced up into the side of a car with a sharp clang.

Then he waited.

And waited.

To her credit, the girl stayed still ten paces behind him and didn't make a sound. When Peter had decided that there were none of them in the immediate area, he beckoned her forwards and climbed the style to cross the fence. Turning to her, he saw that she had reached the part where she had to throw one leg over and was stuck, lacking the strength or confidence to tackle the obstacle with the bag in her had. Wordlessly, Peter reached out for the bag and took it, then froze in surprise as she held her hand out to him, even after he had taken her burden.

He met her eyes and reached out to take her hand, feeling her warm, little fingers grip his as she climbed the rest of the way over. She took back the bag from his hand without being asked to and looked up at him expectantly. He nodded, then walked to the nearest house where he found both doors locked, but a small window to the kitchen open. He slipped off his bag and tried to climb up to it, but he couldn't gain any purchase with his feet to do anything other than look inside.

The house was empty, and more importantly it had no

musty smell that the ones trapped inside made. Pulling a face of disappointment as he climbed back down, he heard a small noise. Looking at the girl, he watched as she made the noise again, a small and deliberate cough in her throat, and pointed a finger at her chest.

The finger was then pointed at the window, and Peter finally understood. He held up a finger of his own to signal that she should wait, then used the prongs of his pitchfork to tap loudly on the window to be doubly sure that there was nothing nasty inside. Repeating the process and finding no good reason to turn down her offer of help, he slipped off his back pack and rested his pitchfork against the back door. He awkwardly held out his hands to her, silently asking for permission to pick her up, and she stepped into his hands.

Given that there was only a relatively small age difference between them, Peter struggled to lift her, but she eventually managed to get her hands onto the open frame. Now that she held some of her own weight, he managed to push her upwards to watch as she threw one short leg into the gap and slipped inside. He watched as she climbed carefully down from the kitchen worktop and disappeared from view as she went towards the door. He waited, but the door didn't open. Fear rising inside him, he was about to knock and shout to her or climb back to the window to see if she was still there when a noise from inside made him press his ear to the wood of the door and listen.

It sounded like a creaking noise at first, then grew louder with each interval as it sounded, then paused. Just as Peter's brain registered what it was, the door clicked and unlocked from inside, only for the door to swing open and bump into the chair she had dragged over to be able to reach the release latch.

Peter snatched up the bags and his pitchfork and slipped

inside as she pulled the chair away, beaming a shy smile at her ingenuity.

"That was really clever," Peter told her in a whisper as he closed and locked the door again, before reaching up to slip across the bolt that most houses had on their doors. She smiled again, then her face dropped back into neutral as he told her to wait in the kitchen while he searched the house.

Every step he took was mirrored. She let him get four steps ahead, then began to follow, copying his every gesture as she carried an imaginary pitchfork behind him. Peter didn't notice, not until he had searched the lounge and turned to see her dogging his steps. He smiled, said nothing, and continued to clear the house, knowing that she was following him.

As he climbed the stairs, he stepped exaggeratedly from one side to the other, bobbing his head like a disco dancer with each step. He heard the slight breath of an almost silent giggle from behind him, which made him smile. Each room they went into, he closed the curtains slowly, keeping the movement gentle so as to not attract attention. By the time they had searched the second bedroom, the girl automatically went to close the other curtain to the one Peter held, and he reminded her to do it slowly and carefully. She nodded, being extra careful to do as she was told.

Peter stopped creeping, stood upright and held the pitchfork in a relaxed way to signify that the house was safe, then beckoned her to follow him downstairs to where he used a chair to stand on and assess the haul from the cupboards.

It wasn't much, but the tap still yielded some cold water. Peter used a can opener to take the lid off a tin of beans and slid it over to the girl who sat opposite him at the table. She picked up the spoon he had laid out for her and, with occasional glances back at him, ate the entire contents.

When they had both finished, to add to the dried snot and general grime on her face, the tomato sauce had got all over her mouth and chin. Peter dabbed a tea towel in the cold water he had run into the sink and asked permission with his eyes to clean her up. She scrunched up her nose, making him laugh, and squirmed on instinct as he wiped away the filth on her face. When he had finished, he gave her a china cup of water and sat back down with her.

"I'm called Amber," she said in a small voice, "and I'm almost four and three-quarters."

TEN

Sergeant Horton, commander of fifty percent of the assorted group's heavy armour in the form of the Chieftain main battle tank employed to block the perilous road bridge onto the island, called out for his driver to roll forwards.

The defences were set so that the slab-sided rear of the tank served as a heavily armed barricade, with two machine guns and the ridiculous overkill of the 120mm cannon pointing back towards the mainland separated only by a strip of fast-moving coastal water. Already, given their initial burst of adrenaline from the large-scale deployment to bring order back to the streets of London, they had encountered a new enemy, terrifying, if not also vulnerable in many ways. That enemy had sparked flight, then a near suicidal tactic to protect the others on the island, and now boredom.

For a month now, he had taken turns with the other men trained to fight from within the confines of one of the finest tanks in creation, and he was reduced to being a very heavy, very expensive, bouncer. He guarded the door, rolling their tank forwards and backwards for the faster vehicles to roll out and find gainful employment, and he was bored.

Although not yet rostered to be on duty, he had risen early due to the noise that all the men readying to depart had made, and he could not get back to sleep, so he took his turn early on the bridge. He watched the four vehicles leave, wishing that he could be a part of something useful, or at least more useful than he felt sitting still all day. He did very little all day other than watch the ground in the distance for any movement, although he was relieved for a short break around midday. Hearing via the radio that the marines were due back, he had the tank started, ready to roll it forward before the two Saxons came into view with their angular, squat faces looking intimidating as they crossed the bridge. Shortly afterwards, he repeated the orders and watched as the other two new additions, the identical armoured personnel carriers, then he rolled back into place. Following that, the sight and sound of the two helicopters washed over him from high on the island behind him, where there was sufficient space near the exposed lighthouse to land the aircraft. Keeping his discipline and not watching the show in the direction of safety, he kept his eyes ahead on the direction of danger, despite his boredom.

As the final four, the original vehicles of the mission returned, he gave the orders for the last time and glanced back at the back end of the light tank squeaking past on its tracks.

His brain took a few precious seconds to fully understand what he was looking at. At first, given the acceptable colours and patterns of the thing, he assumed it was army kit slung on the outside of their wagon, as was the way of things.

But the way it hung was wrong. The way it had a head, and a face, and the way it turned that face to bear its teeth at the noisy tank as it went past, was suddenly so terrifyingly wrong.

Horton began to shout, to scream a pointless warning as the combined noise made by so many large engines drowned him out completely. He waved his arms frantically, pausing only for a second to consider opening up with the machine gun on the back of the tank, and dismissing that as the hatches were open and the head and shoulders of the commander were exposed. Just above the thing holding on, in their direct line of sight and hence the direction of any bullets they fired, were the two soft-skinned trucks that would be obliterated by their gunfire. Horton continued to scream and wave, deciding in the end to snatch up the sub-machine gun and jump down from the tank to land heavily on the roadway. Running as fast as he could with a partly numb ankle caused by the uncontrolled drop, he threw his body after the convoy and fired a short burst of automatic shots into the water beside him in desperation to attract the attention of the man with his back to the danger.

Just as the convoy slowed to play nice with the RMP roadblock and follow their orders to go into search and quarantine, the men in front noticed something behind was wrong.

As his wagon came to a juddering stop, Corporal Ashdown glanced behind him, just in time to see a mostly fingerless and dead hand swing forwards and latch onto the collar of his smock to drag him backwards.

He yelled out loud in fright, unable to summon the strength in his abdominal muscles to pull both his and the upper body of his attacker back upright. Broken and bloody hands tore at him from within army camouflaged uniform sleeves, and his confusion that one of his own men would do this temporarily blinded him to the priorities. Just as his brain engaged sufficient muscle-memory to reach for his bayonet, the teeth clamped down hard onto his shoulder and lanced pain through his body like a cold knife.

Ashdown screamed, heard what he thought was a distinct crack of bone, and slipped backwards from the Spartan to tumble end over end off the side and to the road below.

Miraculously, Horton had covered the hundred-yard distance despite his twisted ankle and arrived before even the men of the checkpoint had responded to what was happening. Given the speed with which events had unfolded, he hadn't had time to fix his bayonet to his weapon, so instead he reversed it as he half-ran, half-hobbled, to swing the folding stock like a club into the side of the head of the thing.

The scene before him stayed in his mind, stuck there like a macabre freeze-frame that would never leave him. He looked down on a trooper, pulled bodily from his tank without warning, who had half of a soldier − literally, the top half of the body − pushed away from his face with both hands as he screamed repeatedly, stopping only for gasps of air. The half a soldier tried to crane forward, to snap its teeth down, and to try and take a piece of him. It didn't have legs, so it couldn't gain enough purchase to bear down on its intended meal. Broken, ragged fingers clawed at him, scoring deep, bloody marks down his face and neck until Horton caught up to the desperate scramble for survival and caved in the right side of the rotting skull.

He hit it like a cricketer stepping into a fast bowl to send the ball high into the stands. The sound that accompanied the swing was less leather on willow and resoundingly more metal on skull. The crunch of the impact and the answering squelch of the twice-dead corpse hitting the roadway beside Ashdown stopped the screaming and left a ringing silence of frozen inactivity.

That inactivity was shattered by the arrival of the Squadron Sergeant Major, who jogged onto the scene and bellowed orders to stir men into action and usefulness.

"Get that bloody barricade secured," he shouted, pointing ahead to the tank that still hadn't returned to its blocking position, "You lot, get into search and quarantine. Sergeant Swift?"

"Sir," came the acknowledgement from somewhere behind him.

"I'll trouble you to expedite matters, if you don't mind?" he asked pointedly, as everyone else heard the polite phraseology for, 'hurry up and do your fucking job without me having to remind you'.

"Horton," Johnson said through a heaving chest, only now showing that the mad dash downhill had left him in need of oxygen, "help me get him inside."

"But, Sir," Horton responded uncertainly, "the standing orders…"

"Yes, Sergeant," Johnson snarled quietly for just Horton to hear, "*my* standing orders are to search returning soldiers for injuries and quarantine them for a time. The order to," he hesitated as he looked down at his corporal, who was wide-eyed in shock and terror, "render them safe is only when infection is confirmed."

With that, he hauled Ashdown to his feet and Horton spurred himself to assist. The man was breathing rapidly but neither man could feel his skin burning hot beneath his clothing yet. They bundled him into a room of a nearby building which had been cleared for the purpose of quarantining returning men, and they laid him down on the table.

"Out," Johnson ordered the young military policeman stationed there, not turning to watch as the boy fled gratefully.

"You're alright, son," Johnson repeated as he fumbled to remove the webbing and strip his smock and undershirt away. Ashdown said nothing as the two men worked together, roughly pulling his uniform off him. He had dropped into a kind of catatonic state, eyes wide but unseeing and unresponsive.

"There," Horton said, pointing at his right shoulder and taking an involuntary step backwards. Johnson looked and saw livid bruising already forming over his collar bone.

"Get a medic," he said, sensing Horton hesitate a fraction of a second before leaving the room. "You're alright, son," he said again.

The door burst open and Horton returned with one of the marines who was fumbling free a medical kit from his pack. Horton had clearly used his initiative and the authority of his rank to remove a quarantined soldier, rationalising that the man was only going to another quarantined area.

"What have we got?" the marine said, his broad Midlands accent filling the room.

"Nasty bruising on his shoulder, and deep scratches to his face and neck," Johnson responded.

"Has the rest of him been checked?" the marine asked, "For bites, I mean?"

Johnson said nothing but began to untie and remove the man's boots as the others helped to strip him totally naked and turn him this way and that to check every part of his body.

"He's fine," said the marine, "just those two wounds." He thought out loud as he clamped a large hand down on Ashdown's forehead, "What's his name?"

Johnson thought for a second, feeling that annoyance everybody experienced when known information escaped them the same second it was asked for.

"Ashdown," he said after a pause that made him look as though he didn't know his own men, "Graham Ashdown, Corporal," he added, unnecessarily giving the man's rank when it was visible on the arms of his uniform smock.

"Okay Graham, can you hear me, mate?" the marine asked as he peered into his eyes. Johnson stole a glance himself, expecting to see the eyeballs turning milky and blinking, when he realised they were not.

Ashdown mumbled in response as he seemed to come around.

"Didn't go through," he said weakly, his voice cracking as he spoke, "bite didn't go through."

"He's right, you know," the marine said, "this bruising isn't teeth marks, it's something else."

"His webbing straps," Horton said as logic descended on him, "the thing bit him on the strap and just pinched him."

"I think it did more than that," the marine answered as he worked, "the bugger's fractured the bone, I think."

Johnson and Horton both winced at the thought of the pain that would bring the man, but the marine's next words sobered their thoughts.

"These scratches are nasty," he said worryingly, "and likely to cause infection."

Johnson froze, levelled the man with a stare and asked him precisely what he meant by infection.

"Sepsis. Blood poisoning. That kind of thing?" the man said dismissively, making the two men relax until his next words brought them back to a harsh reality again. "But there's always the risk that the other kind of infection might be passed this way…"

The silence hung heavy once more before the marine spoke again.

"Help me make him comfortable," he said, indicating a stack of sheets on a dresser.

Making Ashdown 'comfortable' actually meant tying him down to the table by wrapping the sheets around him and leaving only the upper chest, neck and head exposed. The marine periodically checked Ashdown's temperature with a flat hand on his forehead, and each time he didn't detect any sudden rise. That wasn't to say, conclusively, that the infection wasn't there and spreading at a lower rate than they had seen before.

"I'll take it from here, Sir," the marine said as he prepared to clean and dress the long gouges in the injured man's flesh, "if you could just make sure there's a man on the other side of the door?"

Johnson nodded and turned to leave, then swung back.

"Thank you, Marine," he said in a voice full of genuine meaning, "What's your name?"

"Sealey, Sir," he answered, then Johnson turned back to the door to leave.

Outside, Johnson and Horton both drew in long breaths and turned to see Sergeant Swift and his corporal approaching.

"Sir, Sergeant," he said formally, "if you'll both come with me, please?"

Johnson stopped dead and stared at the man.

"I beg your pardon, Sergeant?" he asked icily.

"Sir," Swift began awkwardly, "your own orders. You've both been exposed to one of them and you need to go into quarantine, just a few hours until we know there aren't any problems..." he trailed off, hoping that good sense would prevail, and the big warrant officer wouldn't tear him apart in front of most of his men. Johnson tensed for a moment as the temporary indecision raged inside him, then he abruptly relaxed and seemed to soften slightly.

"Quite right, Sergeant," he said with a false smile, before turning to Horton and asking, "Shall we?" then setting off back to the room they had just vacated.

"Sir," Swift said hesitantly, a hint of warning creeping into his tone and setting Johnson off as he hoped he wouldn't.

The SSM rounded on him, towering above him by only a few inches but utterly dominating the much younger man.

"Sergeant," he growled, "I am playing along and putting myself into quarantine for a few hours, but I am *not* going into the main hall where my men can become stressed and worried about my being in there," he said as he stepped slowly towards the man, forcing him to pace backwards to avoid the slow collision, "Furthermore," he went on in a more insistent tone, "I'm not going back to my men under these circumstances without definitive news regarding the wellbeing of Corporal Ashdown. Is that understood?"

Swift swallowed and nodded, standing very still as Johnson turned and walked back into the room they had vacated, and closed the door behind them.

"And fetch the Captain," he shouted through the door after it had banged shut.

Marine Sealey looked up at them, seemed to understand quickly and shrugged before returning to his ministering of Ashdown's wounds.

"Need a hand?" Horton asked him, seeing the marine simply shake his head as he concentrated.

With nothing better to do, Johnson and Horton found chairs and settled in for the wait.

————

The afternoon grew dark as unexpected rain clouds billowed in from the direction of the sea. Peter and Amber had brought down thick duvets from the beds upstairs to make themselves comfortable dens on the two settees arranged so that they were facing one another. Strangely, the house didn't have a television set, but the large radio and collection of records arranged under the turntable showed that at least whoever lived there wasn't totally boring.

The bedrooms, only two of them, seemed almost unlived in, and one of them had no personal touches at all, which made Peter think it was a guest bedroom. Applying logic and all that he knew about the world, he decided that a woman lived there on her own. It had to be a woman, he knew, because things were too neat and orderly for it to be a man living alone.

There were all sorts of treats and chocolate bars hidden away in kitchen cupboards and the two children smiled at each other as they ate them. Even better, there were glass bottles of fizzy drinks which needed a bottle opener to free their sugary goodness, and the two of them drank and took turns to let out burps as though it were some kind of competition.

As that amusement wore off, a sudden noise at the back door made both of them jump. Despite Amber's young age, she didn't cry out in fright, but Peter's heart raced so that he was forced to slow his breathing down. He was the protector now, and he felt fear in a way like no other when he had only been responsible for his own life. He rose up, keeping his body low as he snatched up the pitchfork that was never far from his reach. Edging towards the back door, he paused to listen, hearing nothing, and just as he began to relax, something erupted from the dull light outside the window to launch itself through the gap.

Claws scratched and scrabbled at the glass and the frame, and wide, yellow eyes bore into Peter's own as he fell backwards with a strangled squawk of fear.

Frozen in situ, half-in and half-out of the narrow gap, a mottled black and brown cat glared at him with accusatory indignation. It kept its eyes on him, squeezing the rest of its body through as it landed lightly on the kitchen worktop and let out a low yowling sound in his direction.

As foolish as he felt, Peter got the impression that he was being asked a question, and as foolish as he sounded even to himself, he answered it.

"We just needed somewhere safe to stay," he told the cat in a low voice, then jumped again as the cat dropped down from the worktop without warning and paced past him to trot towards the settees. He turned to see it had its tail held high and vertical with the top curled around like it was a living question mark. Even from three paces away he could hear the deep, percussive rattle of the cat's purring as it nuzzled Amber, before rising on its back legs to rub one side of its whiskers along her outstretched hand. She giggled lightly, and the cat turned to repeat the gesture on the other side of its face before hopping up effortlessly to nuzzle her face and knead the duvet on her lap.

Feeling distinctly as though he was the intruder, the items he had discarded before in the kitchen came back to him. He had ignored the tins of cat food as an irrelevance, as though the thought of any animal surviving had been pushed from his mind, after the dog he had tried so hard to forget about.

The obvious evidence to the contrary had now settled down and begun a rigorous washing process on Amber's lap, pausing occasionally to lick her hand when it came close enough, and made her giggle again.

Peter felt suddenly ashamed, as though he had broken into the house of someone who was still around, because the cat evidently lived there.

He opened a tin from the kitchen and scraped out the foul-smelling contents onto a side plate. As soon as the can opener sang its metallic tune to cut off the top, the cat abandoned its cleaning ritual and bounded up onto the side, where it snaked its way in between Peter's hands until the meal was prepared. Leaving the plate on the side, they both watched as the cat ate hungrily, purring the whole time and surprising him that such feline ventriloquism was even possible. Finishing the entire plate and licking the jelly residue clean, the cat promptly stepped back to the windowsill and leapt up to squeeze itself back outside.

Peter glanced back to Amber, seeing her expression fall back into the sadness he had known previously. He tried to cheer her up with more chocolate, which didn't work. He tried drinking more of the fizzy drink and pulled faces as he burped musically but she stayed crestfallen at the loss of something that had made her happy.

Giving in, Peter settled down to sleep on the settee and drifted away trying to think of ways to keep her safe and happy.

ELEVEN

Life below the waves was a claustrophobic, dank, stifling existence of enforced silence. Any man over five and a half feet tall suffered from constant spinal issues given any amount of time spend on board a boat, but the long journey around the Horn of Africa and back north to British waters was made under the strictest insistence that the journey remained covert. That meant that the submarine could only surface when absolutely necessary, and the remainder of the time had to be spent running quietly.

The four men who were the precious cargo of the route, all of them sporting wild beards beneath staring eyes, had little to do besides lay in their cramped berths and wait for the journey to be over, but then men of their experience were not known for complaining about hardship.

Their commander, Major Clive Downes, was the newest man to the regiment and would be forced to rotate out at some point in the future, or at least he would have under normal circumstances, but he had no idea what would happen, given this latest development.

He and his team had been in Afghanistan, unofficially of

course, and had been teaching the rag-tag collection of goat herders and illiterate villagers the finer points of improvised explosive device manufacture and planning, in addition to delivering the manual on the American-made and supplied Stinger missile system.

The Soviets had officially ceased hostilities in the country after a decade of vicious counter-insurgency had left the region a war-torn mess, and that war had cost the Russians dearly. It was already widely known amongst the military as Russia's own Vietnam.

The fighting of enemies via a proxy was nothing new, and it was a badly-kept secret that the west was supplying and supporting the insurgents as a way to chip away at the iron curtain without getting their own hands dirty. At least not publicly, anyway.

Downes had received orders, bizarrely through the channels of the Royal Navy, and he had followed those orders, which led him and the three men under his command to be sharing the same stale air in a submarine compartment barely big enough for their equipment. Any questions he had thought to ask were cut off, as the orders were given with a resounding, "out" at the end. The four Americans working alongside them, each going by an obviously false moniker, were also extracted via the same strategy, but they saw little of them on the journey, and guessed they had been whisked away to report to their CIA masters as soon as they surfaced.

Now, three weeks after those orders had led them to half suffocate and suffer from vitamin D deficiency, they arrived in a very unseasonably stormy English Channel.

———

"Sergeant Major?" came the polite, well-mannered enquiry through the closed door.

"Sir?" Johnson answered, thinking that his orders for the captain to be fetched had been followed, and instead finding that the man himself had not come, but had sent his younger brother.

"Sergeant Major, I must ask after your health," said Second Lieutenant Palmer, "Are you quite well?"

"Fine, Lieutenant, thank you," Johnson replied gruffly, "we'll be out of here in an hour, don't you worry."

"Quite," Palmer chuckled, implying that Johnson's welfare was the slightest bit concerning to him personally. "Compliments from the Captain, but when you're ready he'd rather enjoy hearing from you about the events of this afternoon."

I bet he bloody would, Johnson thought to himself, biting back the retort that the Captain, last time he checked, had two working legs and was quite capable of walking his royal arse down there and asking the question in person.

"Very good, Lieutenant," Johnson said instead, using the prinked boy's lowly rank instead of inflating his ego further with another 'Sir'.

"Oh," the officer said from outside in afterthought, "and how is our man?"

Johnson took a breath again before answering, just in case the words he was thinking came out of his mouth instead of the words he should say.

"Corporal Ashdown is stable, and there are no signs that he is infected," Johnson said.

"But we haven't encountered, er, *injuries* such as this before, have we?" he responded, letting Johnson know that the facts must be common knowledge, but that Palmer was actually questioning why the injured man had been brought inside their cordon. "No,' Johnson said, "we haven't."

The sound of boots marching away in a relaxed tempo made the SSM's blood boil, making him breach his own standing orders and leave the room with thirty minutes to go before the allotted time. Despite the fact that nobody else had been removed from quarantine, he was storming up the hill unchallenged when he noticed the royal military police sergeant duck into a doorway to avoid having to lie if asked later if he had seen the SSM. Johnson banged into the headquarters building and startled the men inside, finding a scene of intense business and stress, instead of the relaxed atmosphere he was expecting.

Captain Palmer was sitting in front of one of the radio sets, one earphone cupped to the side of his head and scribbling furiously with a pencil on a pad of paper before him. His shirt-sleeves were rolled up and he appeared red-eyed as though he hadn't stopped to blink in the last two hours.

Guiltily, Johnson regretted his malice towards the man for sending his younger brother when he clearly had important things to do. He was wordlessly handed a tin mug holding a hot drink so freshly made that it burned his hand and forced him to change his grip. He waited patiently as he watched Captain Palmer acknowledge transmissions curtly and efficiently, without pausing in his insistent writing. He finished the call and handed the headset back to corporal Mander, who was on duty. Climbing to his feet wearily and rubbing his eyes, the officer also accepted a drink but was staring at the paper before him so intently that he didn't flinch at the heat of his own mug. Appearing to only just notice the Sergeant Major, he put down both paper and drink to shake his hand and place his left on the strong shoulder opposite him.

"Mister Johnson, I'm glad you are safe," he said with genuine gratitude for the man's survival. "How is Ashdown? He's Maxwell's 2ic, isn't he?" he asked, showing that he had either been passed that information recently or had rapidly absorbed this knowledge about his adopted and partly-manned squadron of Yeomanry. Johnson suspected it was the latter.

"Stable, Sir, thank you," he said, "he's showing no sign of…

of *turning*, and he's under the care of one of the marines' medics."

"Excellent," Palmer said with passion behind his eyes, "I'm sure he'll pull through. Now," he said, changing the subject after sufficient time as to not appear callous regarding the lives of his men, "C.A.S. have been on the blower. They are calling themselves that now, Command at Sea, apparently, and it's all above board with government and all branches of the military." He paused to offer time for questions but continued as Johnson clearly had none. "They are in the process of consolidating military assets all over the place. It's mostly bad news, I'm afraid…" he paused to blow on the surface of the drink he had picked up, only now seeming to find it hot to touch.

"And what do they have for us?" Johnson asked, reading between the lines and guessing that the scribbled notes were the bones of a mission.

"Nothing for now," he said excitedly, "it seems as though we are one of the rare pockets with a good number of civilian refugees. They want to add to us here and are directing what personnel they can to get to our location. Others will be our responsibility to bring back."

"Okay," Johnson said simply, feeling drained and unable to think about anything else, given the day's activities so far.

Graham Ashdown slept until the sky outside was fully dark.

Everyone had endured their quarantine countdown in subdued quiet after the unexpected events of their arrival. The search process was simplified, given that soldiers had few qualms over being naked in front of their peers. Each man had stripped, ready to be examined and the method evolved organically so that the RMPs got all of the marines and soldiers through quickly, and they were able to get comfortable and settle in to wait.

The story of what had happened ran through the men like only a rapidly-spreading rumour could, so that a convoluted version of events now lowered their mood and made for a depressing air. The men all shuffled out when the time was called, and none of them had manifested a fever or even a hint of an elevated temperature. They reported back to their individual billets with their heads down, despite the successes of the day, and the small house remained closed up, with the single soldier standing outside wearing his scarlet beret and an expression of stoic apology.

That soldier was both startled and relieved in the same moment when the Yeomanry Sergeant Major returned. He ordered the door open but thanked him with a tired smile as he stepped inside.

Johnson's heart was heavy as he fully expected to find his man dead. He hoped to hear that he had gone in his sleep. He did not expect to walk in and see Ashdown sitting up, bandages wrapped around his neck, with a tin cup of steaming liquid in one hand and a cigarette in the other. He smiled, despite the pain he was clearly in, and looked at the contents of each hand as though his mind was juggling them to decide which one he should put down so he could stand up.

"Jesus, Graham," Johnson said with wide eyes, "how? What happened?"

This last was directed at marine Sealey, who was stripped down to trousers and T-shirt, with the same contents in his own hand as Ashdown had.

"Slept it off, Sir," he said with a smile, "temperature never got up, even though he was talking a lot in his sleep, but he just came 'round, like. You're alright now, ain't ya, mate?"

Ashdown watched Sealey as he spoke, then turned back to Johnson wearing the same smile of almost fanatical relief to stutter his own explanation.

"I thought I was a gonner, Sir," he said, the slightest quiver in his chin, "I really thought the scratches would have…"

He sniffed once, getting a grip of himself before the stress and realisation of almost dying and worse, threatened to unravel him, then carried on with bright eyes that tried to over-compensate.

"The shoulder is sore as hell, but I'll be back at it in a few days," he finished.

"You'll be stood down for more than a few days, Ashdown," Johnson chuckled at him, "we need to get you moved somewhere more comfortable. Give you some time off. Your family are here, aren't they?"

"My missus and my boy, yes, Sir," he said as his face darkened slightly, and he coughed to clear his voice, "they're billeted with Sergeant Maxwell's family."

His face stayed shrouded in worry, as though the mention of his family gave a sharp reminder of what he had to lose. Johnson recognised that the man had been through enough, more than enough, and told him to rest up. His eyes met the marine's and the slight flick of his head summoned him to follow outside.

"Stay where you are, mate," he told Ashdown as he set his drink on the table and slipped the rolled-up cigarette back in his mouth, "I'm going to see if any of my muckers are about to help."

Outside, and a good few paces away from the house, marine and warrant officer stood in momentarily awkward silence as both sought the appropriate words.

"You have my thanks," Johnson said, wincing at what he felt was an overly formal tone. He meant the words, however, and was truly grateful that his man wasn't dead or worse.

Marine Sealey shrugged away the heartfelt words noncha-lantly, not sharing his own fears that the man he didn't know wouldn't wake and he would be forced to put him down. That would have potentially pushed the subtle enmity between marines and squaddies to boil closer to the surface, if only he and a dead man had known the truth of things. But luckily, that had not happened.

"It must be only the teeth, I reckon," he told Johnson.

"The teeth?"

"Yeah, I mean, the scratches didn't infect him, not with the Screecher virus or whatever anyway, and the teeth didn't break the skin, so I reckon it's something about the teeth," he explained simply before adding a warning, "But he'll definitely need some antibiotics; God knows what shit has got into him otherwise."

"I'll pass that up, thanks," Johnson told him, then asked if he was okay to sort moving Ashdown to where his family was temporarily living.

"I think your mate has ideas there, Sir," he said, pointing to the approaching sergeant Maxwell, "If you don't need me anymore, mind if I find my oppos?" he asked hopefully, meaning his friends and fellow marines.

"No, thanks again, marine," Johnson said and offered him a hand.

Sealey shook it, replying, "No problem, I'm hanging after lashing up your Pongo," he finished with a goading grin before trotting off to find his 'oppos'.

Johnson smiled at the liberal use of marine slang, which he suspected was either partly for his benefit, or that marine Sealey had joined young and been transformed into the rare beast of a Royal Marine Commando and embraced their unique language as his own.

Maxwell joined him and asked, "Did that Bootneck just call us Pongos?"

"Yep," Johnson replied with amusement, smirking at the marine's name for the apparently foul-smelling soldiers of the British Army.

"If it ain't bad enough with the arabs…" Maxwell said,

using their own inside terminology meaning Arrogant Regular Army Bastards. The rift between the regulars and the reservists, although not noticeable since the brief bar fight, had not come to a head for one simple reason in Johnson's opinion; there were more reservists than regulars to make it a fair fight. He had hoped that the kind of territorial pissing contests of different military units and branches in one confined space wouldn't affect them, given the unprecedented depth of shit they found themselves in, but it seemed that wasn't to be the case.

The marines were fine. They were led by a competent officer and sergeant and while they kept themselves to themselves, they weren't hostile in the slightest.

And besides, he thought to himself, *I'd be worried if there wasn't a bit of inter-service piss-taking.*

"Anyway," Johnson said as he snapped out of his small reveries and changed the subject, "Ashdown says his family is with yours, that right?"

"Yes," he answered simply, then frowned and turned to Johnson with wide eyes, "What? He spoke?"

"He's fine, Simon," Johnson told him, "said Bootneck reckons he'll need antibiotics, but the thing didn't manage to bite him. He's still himself."

"Sir," Maxwell acknowledged as he simultaneously excused himself to run to the door and throw it open.

Johnson smiled, knowing that the man would be cared for, but reminding himself that he should be watched closely by someone with a bayonet handy until he was fully restored. He wandered to the building used as both the guard house, as it was the closest to the bridge, and because it was large enough to accommodate their sleeping needs it was also the billet for the Monkeys, or RMPs, seeing as they were neck-deep in unofficial terminology.

Johnson found Swift, the beleaguered sergeant, and

decided not to add the pressure of guarding an injured man located higher up the island to his list of worries.

"Good work earlier," he told him, not sure if he meant with the main quarantine work or because he'd had the balls to tell Johnson himself that he had to follow the rules. Swift nodded his acceptance of the ambiguous compliment and watched as Johnson turned to walk back uphill to find the headquarters building.

There he found Palmer sitting beside the radio operator, who was now Corporal Daniels, having evidently replaced Mander at the shift change organised by another of his reliable NCOs. Palmer leaned back in the chair to stretch his aching spine as Johnson walked in, offering him a tired smile of welcome.

"All is well, I trust, Mister Johnson?" he asked.

"It is, Sir," he responded as he glanced around the room for anything hot and wet to ease his throat, "Ashdown's recovered."

Palmer sat bolt upright and fixed him with an excited look. Keeping his eyes on the SSM, he spoke over his shoulder politely to Daniels.

"Corporal, I'll keep an ear on the radio, would you mind fetching up a brew from somewhere?"

Daniels acknowledged him, rising to leave the room as he had clearly been ordered to act as servant and told to leave the room because the grown-ups were talking. But he did so happily because Captain Palmer had a way of getting people to do things without ordering them about.

"Fully recovered?" Palmer asked. "No infection from the bite?"

"No bite," Johnson said as he scraped chair legs on the floor to spin a seat around to face the officer, "the thing cracked his collarbone, but it bit him on the webbing strap and didn't break the skin. The scratches were a concern, but they don't seem to have spread the disease."

"Interesting," Palmer said as he put forefinger and thumb of his right hand to his top lip and picked in absent-minded gentleness, "and where is he now?"

"Sergeant Maxwell is going to set him up in the billet where their families are, and I'm going to have a man with him at all times until he's recovered."

Palmer nodded enthusiastically, glad that Johnson had evidently pre-empted his thoughts on the risk still remaining.

"The marine who patched him up did a good job, but he doesn't have the antibiotics we need," Johnson went on hopefully, "Any chance we could ask our new command structure for a doctor and supplies?"

Palmer mused for a moment, opening his mouth once and closing it again as though he changed his mind about what he was going to say. He went to speak again but the door banged open and both men turned to see Daniels backing his way into the room using his backside to push the door ahead of him. He pivoted on the spot to reveal the two mugs in his hands before crossing the room and looking at each hand to decide which drink was which. His frown remained as he glanced between the left and right mugs, then handed one to each man. Daniels left the room, no doubt to retrieve his own drink and slip outside to smoke in peace and stretch his back.

Both men bent their faces to the mugs, unable to differentiate between the strong, dark liquids by sight but smelling that they had each other's drinks.

Johnson passed the tea with two sugars to Palmer, who in turn passed over the coffee with two to Johnson.

"I'm waiting for them to get back to me," he told the SSM conspiratorially, "and that's one of the things they are sending. The other is a new boss for all of us."

TWELVE

Ellie and Pauline kept quiet company, in the intervals when Ellie wasn't crying pitifully for the loss of her daughter, screaming murder at their captors or sleeping off the blow to her head. The older woman tried to hush her, to comfort her, but she hadn't spoken a single conscious word for three days, other than to promise every vengeance known to mankind if they didn't take her back to get her daughter.

When the tears finally ran out, when the crippling acceptance sunk into Ellie's mind, she became nearly catatonic. Pauline had initially misunderstood her when she had cried over the loss of her baby, assuming that the young woman, like so many, had seen loved ones pulled down and killed by the devil that now inhabited the bodies of the infected. After the rants against the guards, after the pleading to be allowed to go back and find her, she finally plucked up the courage to risk upsetting her and ask the question.

"She isn't dead, is she? Isn't one of them?" she asked the girl.

Ellie sniffed and turned her red, emotionless eyes towards her and stared, then rolled away. Pauline sat back, not wanting to push the issue any further, but the voice sounded low and soft from the bed opposite her own.

"We hid in the house for almost a week," she said in a flat voice that croaked after the effort of her screams and tears, "we stayed upstairs, kept quiet, and I taught my baby not to cry and make a noise."

She sniffed, pushed herself upright and cuffed at her face with both sleeves pulled over her hands. Sitting up and tucking her heels into her thighs, she hugged her knees tightly.

"A massive crowd of them came through," she went on, her eyes staring at a spot of nothing on the floor, "they literally shook the houses there were so many of them. More of them came on behind for about a day, like they were late to the party, and two of them must have smelled us or something because they camped outside and just kept walking into the front door like it would magically open for them. I threw a load of things out of the back window, you know, to try and get them to go away, and it worked. The microwave made a massive noise and they loved that. It gave us just enough time to get out of the front door and into the car…"

She sniffed again, wiping away the fresh tears of memory with her cuffs.

"We got about two miles out of town when I ran over a few of them at once and the car got stuck. We had to run and leave the car."

She stopped talking, never taking her eyes away from the spot she was staring at, as if it was the invisible anchor tethering her to reality no matter how harsh it was. Pauline waited to see if the pause was an intentional one, then decided to prompt for more.

"What happened?"

Ellie's head snapped up to meet Pauline's gaze, startling her slightly with her sudden alertness and a fire behind her eyes that quickly extinguished itself.

"What happened?" she spat. "We were doing fine, that's what happened. We moved around a short distance at a time and Am…" the word, the name, seemed to catch in her throat, "my baby was doing really well; she never made a noise to attract them. Then these," she pushed herself up on her hands and shouted, "*fucking bastards*, came and dragged me away from her."

She buried her head into her knees and sobbed again for a long time until the reserves of tears ran dry again. She raised her head, the same vacant, capitulating look in her eyes.

"My beautiful baby, my Amber, she's gone now. There's no way she'd be able to survive on her own," she intoned flatly.

Pauline didn't know what to say, but blessedly the door banged open and a man stood in the doorway.

"Time for work," he said, leering as Pauline stood and smoothed down her clothes. As she passed by, she reached out a hand and placed the lightest touch of her fingertips on Ellie's knee.

―――――

Pauline Earle, widow and manager at a historical site with its own hotel, had been rounded up early on after the world fell apart. She had survived the initial phase of apocalyptic proceedings on simple geography, sheer luck alone, as her modest home was part of the hotel-cum-museum on the windswept seafront on high ground far from the town. She'd lived there ever since her husband had passed away, selling their house and accepting the job with its accommodation and company. There, she'd anxiously watched the news reports as she sat alone on the day when only two of the employees arrived for work to care for the single pair of guests present.

In her unthinking panic, she had stopped off via the village shop a few miles from her home, and for a week she lived on the overstocked amount of bread and milk that her subconscious brain forced her to buy.

She had nothing to drink in the house, not that she ever drank much anyway, and wouldn't think of going to the hotel wing to drink their stocks. The stress of the situation made her think of turning to alcohol for a solution. It was probably a good idea she hadn't found anything, as that night she saw the first one of them. Had she drunk most of a bottle of wine as she'd felt like doing, she probably would have gone outside to investigate and ask why they were trespassing. She probably wouldn't have noticed the curious way they were walking, their jerky movements and the way that the head snatched from side to side whenever different sounds echoed around her little hilltop haven. That decision not to drink, the possession of her full faculties, inevitably saved her life as she made the choice not to go out there. She had stayed frozen still in the window and watched as the thing walked up to the glass and banged its face into the rain-smeared pane. Pauline gasped in horror, unable to move through a morbid fascination and fear, and couldn't believe it when a bird flew down to land lightly on the grass nearer the sea. The thing in front of her, wearing a green waterproof and walking gear with one gaiter torn away above its right boot to show a ragged chunk of blackened flesh missing, turned and watched intently as the bird hopped along. It lurched towards the cliff edge, head cocked to one side and hands reaching out for the pastel-grey dove as it went about its business, undisturbed by events unfolding in the wider world. It remained utterly undisturbed until almost too late when the sudden burst of movement behind it forced a panicked leap out over the edge of the drop towards the sea and freedom. The person, the *thing*, chasing the dove fell headlong over the edge and made Pauline shriek out loud in shock. She ran outside, lay flat on the damp, windswept grass to peer over the edge and saw the body only thirty feet down and stuck in grotesque parody of a ballerina with legs and arms broken in different directions. The face showed that it recognised her appearance, and a shriek rang from the mouth in between the snapping of teeth. She almost thought to try the telephone again to bring help, until her mind registered what her eyes had seen. The face looked up at her, full of malice and hate, but the body was still face down on the rocks. Only then did she realise what the world was facing.

Three days passed by without any updates on the static screen of her television, and a nervous young man working in the hotel knocked on the door of her small cottage to ask if she would join them for a meeting. The meeting, such as it was, comprised Pauline and two young local men who worked there, and the couple of guests who had been caught out while on a walking holiday along their famous Jurassic coastline. The silence had been awkward, the introductions stilted, until they started to relax around one another, and they all agreed that they had to shed the bounds of normality and wait at the hotel for the whole unpleasant business to all be over.

That bubble of British stoicism burst spectacularly when one morning about a week after the televisions stopped broadcasting, three men drove arrogantly up to the very front of the main entrance to the visitors' centre of the historical hilltop monument and ruins. They walked around, appearing to be conducting an appraisal, apparently liking what they saw. Pauline looked out of her window, barely able to hear the exchange of words with the two employees who walked out of the front door of the hotel to greet the visitors.

Pleasantries were given and received, hands were shaken, and questions asked.

Questions that, at least in their current suspicious frame of mind, would raise the alarm.

Questions like how many people were there, what supplies they had and what weapons were in the building.

Questions which, when answered, prompted the bearded man loitering by his car to turn and wave his hands in an exaggerated gesture down the hill. The five members of the reluctant group who had yet to realise the cruel world they were now living in watched in confusion. That confusion turned into fear and disbelief as the noise of a loud engine rattled up the hill to them. The throttle surged, whistling and growling in peaks and dipping low to rise up again until the most unexpected sight burst into view.

A tank. A dark green tank with wide, irregular swathes of black and brown painted over it. The tank, so unnatural and out of place in the idyllic setting, was followed by half a dozen other vehicles including two vans and a digger, forming a ragtag collection that oozed danger. The tank stopped, the engine rattled into silence, and a hatch opened to let a man climb out. Everyone watched in terrified awe as he jumped lightly down, holding a machine gun with a long magazine sticking out of the left side horizontally. He held the weapon by the grip in his left hand, letting it swing casually and recklessly. Everything about him screamed a warning of violence and cruelty. As if to compound the implied sense of doom, the man surveyed the area.

And smiled crookedly.

———

The next few weeks were tough. Every room was thoroughly searched and ransacked for the items the half dozen men wanted, and the carefully maintained grounds of the historic site were systematically ruined as the centuries-old defences were deepened and widened in their neat rings which had once been dug to the same depth and width to prevent Vikings from reaching the hill top.

One of the reasons that site was so important, and had

been for as long as humans had graced the south coast, was that the hilltop had its own natural water spring. The Anglo-Saxons of Wessex could hold that hilltop for a fortnight with only two hundred and fifty men, given that they only had to carry their weapons and food on their backs, and they could not be starved out easily. Each day, the besieging army would be forced to raid further and further away for their own food and water.

Each day those besiegers sat impotently at the bottom of the hill meant another boat crew melting away for easier spoils or prompted impatient men into ill-conceived attempts on the steep hill.

Fast forward to their current war, their plight against the violent invaders of today, and the routine had not changed much, other than the defenders now had a small hotel and visitors' centre to keep them comfortable. They also had the added bonus of a vast underground store of heating oil, installed when the visitors' centre had the gift shop added about a decade before.

What they didn't have was a food supply, but the daily runs sent out in cars and vans brought back more than enough, and about one in five outbound cars brought back someone new. Those new people were in varying states of dishevelment, and not all of them seemed totally willing to be there. Anyone coming back in via the single-track road that led up to the ruins and the buildings would find themselves staring down the barrel of the tank for an unnervingly long time.

It wasn't a tank, not in the sense that most people associated with the main battle tanks synonymous with the military might of each country, but it was in fact one of the newly introduced Warrior tracked fighting vehicles. It was a bigger version of the tracked vehicles the Yeomanry used in their assault reconnaissance troop, with the addition of the brutal

30mm cannon from the Fox and a section to carry infantry like the Saxons.

It was better armoured, more mechanically reliable, but it had one flaw according to the man who had driven it there. One small part of the wagon that was inferior to the older vehicles they had been invented to replace. The new chain gun, which fired the same 7.62 as the GPMGs, was prone to jamming and had a far slower rate of fire than the tried and tested weapon it was due to replace.

The man who had driven it there, the man with the machine gun. The one with the cruel eyes who had made the unwilling acquaintance of most of the women there already, who gave his orders to other people to follow, and dished out their rewards like some petty Lord. He didn't mix with many of them, electing instead to stay inside the biggest room in the hotel, which he had taken over as his own space, and he only kept company when he wanted it.

He demanded company, and the implied threat meant that he didn't have to force himself on anyone. They were protected by him. He kept them all safe and they didn't have to go out where the monsters were, but that protection obviously came at a price, which they willingly paid, wearing false smiles so that everything stayed amicable.

Pauline was spared those unwelcome attentions, as there were younger women who caught his eye before her. For that she was both relieved and grateful yet felt guilty and responsible that others had to endure being used when she was left alone.

Michaels. That was what the others called him. He occasionally went out, but other men were left there in charge. None of them would ever think of trying to depose their self-styled leader, mainly because he was the only man who knew things.

Things like how to get into an army camp and find guns.

Things like the exact building that contained a gleaming new tank, and even more miraculously, how to start it up and drive it out. Even more mind-bendingly, he knew where the ammunition was that the cannon took, and after he had stared at the racks where it was stored for a long time and counted the empty sections with his fingers, he selected ones with glossy black tips as he muttered to himself.

He filled the rear section with the two rows of horizontal seats with box upon box of ammunition of various types and calibre. He added to that other pieces of equipment and tools, fitted himself with a belt that had straps over each shoulder and multiple pouches, and drew the bayonet from the sheath to check its edge.

When they were equipped to his requirements and ready to leave the army camp, one of the two men he had recruited to assist him asked, "Why don't we just bust our way out of here?". They were sitting in the rear seats, the position of the gunner and commander, with strict instructions not to touch anything as Michaels drove.

"Because," he said, dragging out the word into the headset that linked them over the rumble and roar of the engine and tracks, "we don't want anyone to know we've been here, and if we need to come back it would be nice if the place wasn't full of dead people because some idiot drove through the gate instead of opening it. Dickhead."

So they had left the camp and the nearby ammunition dump as though nobody had been there, and when the army *had* returned, they failed to notice the missing vehicle and the ammunition taken from the rearmost sections away from the entrance.

Now that Warrior, that dominant vehicle that was impervious to almost anything other than the mighty Chieftain tanks miles away down the coast, sat hidden in the ruins of the old fort, partially obscured by a collapsed wall of heavy stone, and camouflaged the rest of the way using cut branches. Unless anyone approaching in a vehicle knew it was there, they would be well within deadly range of the 30mm cannon for far too long to make any assault anything other than a bloodbath or one-sided losses.

They were nestled in, and they had no intention of being dug out.

THIRTEEN

The first morning they woke up together, the two children sat up and looked at each other awkwardly. They had slept remarkably well given the tumultuous events of the previous day, but the morning air was chilly thanks to the small, high window they had left open during the night.

They hadn't noticed the cold when they slept wrapped up inside a double duvet each, but now that they were out of those cocoons they shivered in the cool air. Still, the cost of leaving that window open was repaid by what it had brought back to them in the darkness.

The yellow eyes, the black and brown mottled fur and its eager, expectant look; the cat stood and stretched up to arch its back, before sitting down and turning its head far to the right to desperately lick behind its own shoulder blade, then stopping just as rapidly to look at them again.

Peter and Amber looked at each other, both wearing small smiles, then back at the cat, who regarded them with its big eyes that closed in slow blinks as the loud rattle of a purr wound itself back up to full volume. Amber held a single finger out to it, giggling as the cat pushed itself forward to rub the entire length of its left side along the digit and spin delicately in front of her face to look at Peter.

This had the unwelcome side effect of placing its back end with the upturned tail directly in Amber's face and making her lean back to move her eyes away from the display. They both laughed softly, and the cat looked at them both in turn to show them it was unimpressed to the extent that it was almost ashamed of them.

Peter had never had a cat, mostly because any cat hanging around the farm would be seen as food by the working dogs that walked obediently at the heels of their masters. He decided that he liked this cat, as presumptuous and intrusive as it was, and held out his own finger towards it. Shuffling the position of all four paws, it carefully balanced to reach out one paw and try to span the expanse between the two settees to step across.

Try as it might, it had no possible way of extending a single paw to bridge the gap of at least two feet and still make it, but that didn't stop the ridiculous, wobbling display of balance until the realisation finally dawned on it and it stepped lightly down to leap back up on Peter's side, and purr loudly as it snaked its body up and down his hand. Both children smiled at the display, not realising that they were being manipulated into providing more food, just as they had done the previous night.

From the cat's perspective, two people had arrived and didn't scream at it and try to catch it, and they fed it. The biggest draw for the cat was that these two, even if they were small, were warm and smelt like people instead of dead things.

Peter stood and stretched, slipping his arms into a sweat-shirt that was too big for him after being liberated from a house he couldn't remember being inside. He stepped lightly over the cold floor of the kitchen and looked over the contents arrayed on the worktop, as he always did when he cleared a house. He found tinned meatballs, cans of soup that promised to be thick and creamy, and dried pasta.

He thought, then stepped quickly and quietly to the stairs, where he carefully peered through the windows front and back to be sure that there were no monsters loitering in the street. He couldn't be sure if any of the houses were nests, like the two he had discovered by bad luck, and only survived through a moment of good luck, but a decent indication of those places was a wide-open front door.

Deciding to risk it, as he was now bizarrely responsible for not only a kid but apparently a cat too, he returned to the kitchen and ran a pan of water from the tap. When the pan was half-full, the water began to cough and splutter from the pipe as though air were trapped in there somehow, and then it stopped altogether. Peter set down the pan and frowned.

Going through the cupboards, he found another container and went to the other tap in the house in the main bathroom upstairs. He managed to fill most of that smaller pan, which in itself was deceptive, since being smaller, it held much less water anyway, and he carried it carefully downstairs.

Amber was watching him in silence, crossing her legs and leaning forward to wear a look of discomfort. Peter saw this, recognised the look, and in that same moment realised that the girl had been conditioned into this violent new world and would not pee without being told it was safe to do so. He held out a hand to her, beckoning her towards him, and pointed her towards the toilet.

"Just don't flush it," he murmured to her.

Peter had faced that quandary himself in the early days. He had flushed the toilet out of habit alone in the first house he had occupied, and was rewarded with three callers at his door within as many minutes. He'd stolen silently out of the back door and reminded himself not to do that again.

A week later he decided to try another method and peed in

a bucket instead. Through trial and error at a couple of houses, he came to study the effects that his bodily functions had on his survivability, and found that the smell of fresh urine outside was about as sensible as flushing the toilet, but if he kept the bucket inside and tipped it into the toilet carefully, or just used the toilet without flushing, then neither the smell nor the noise would bring unwanted attention.

Suffering the eye sting of ammonia from his own pee was an easy trade-off when balanced against having his body torn apart and eaten by people.

Turning on the gas to the stove, he stepped back and struck a long match before leaning his body away to light the burner. It caught with a *whoomph* and he instinctively shook the match in his hand before dropping the smoking stem of thin wood into the sink. He boiled the water, intermittently checking beyond the drawn curtains to be sure that nothing had detected the subtle atmospheric change caused by a pan of water boiling, and he watched Amber from the corner of his eye as she fussed the cat, who was still trying to encourage her to feed it. He tested the pasta, scalding his fingers as he pulled a single piece from the pan to chew it, deciding that it was soft enough. He drained it with some difficulty, then replaced the pan on the burner and opened a can of meatballs to tip the contents in and stir it messily around with a wooden spoon.

When that had warmed through and begun to sizzle and catch on the bottom of the metal, he turned off the gas and let the pan rest while he found two wide china bowls in an off-beige colour with a ringed flower pattern encircling the lip. He selected them a spoon each and set the table, then opened another tin of cat food and used a fork to spread half of the contents out on a small plate of the same pattern and colour.

As soon as the can opener had made its unique sounds on the tin of meatballs, the cat abandoned Amber as though she no longer existed, stepping away so suddenly and without even

a glance of farewell that the girl deflated. It jumped up on the
kitchen worktop and made itself a nuisance until the cat food
was presented on the plate, then followed the boy like he held
in his hand cat ambrosia. Peter placed the cat's dish on the
kitchen table at the head and pulled out a chair before beckoning Amber over. They sat up and ate their mostly-cooked
breakfast of meatballs and pasta shells with the thin tomato
sauce barely covering their portions as the cat ate noisily, sitting
up at the table with them.

It purred as it chomped on the chunks of unidentifiable
smelly goodness and jelly, making more sound than both children combined as they slurped their own food. The cat
finished first, despite its repeat of the ventriloquist act and
remained sitting up to lick its paws and wash its face, while it
seemed to wait for the others to finish. Amber became full
fairly quickly, as did Peter, who had survived for a month on
snacking, and some days didn't get to eat for hours and hours
on end if the houses he had chosen to rest in were poorly
stocked with tinned goods.

Peter rose to take the dishes away, using plates to cover
their bowls for the rest to be eaten later when they had room in
their bellies. The cat seemed to have room for more and
meowed pitifully at him as he stood in the kitchen, until he
relented and scraped out the remainder of the tin and chopped
it up with a fork.

The cat licked the jelly off a chunk for less than half a
minute, then abruptly turned and flashed the circle of light
skin at the base of its tail in Peter's direction as it got down and
trotted to the settee, where it jumped up without invitation to
knead Amber's legs through the duvet again.

You didn't want food then, Peter thought in annoyance, *you
just wanted me to feed you.*

.   .   .

He cleaned up in the kitchen, leaving the dirty pans in the sink and reorganising the supplies he had found in the cupboards, before returning to his settee. The cat, curled into a neat circle with paws and tail tucked in, raised its head and opened both eyes to glare at him as he sat down. Peter was taken aback by the unexpected look of hostility, and watched with his mouth partly open as the cat jumped down and stretched before walking to the kitchen and jumping up to look at the open window as it calculated the precise physics of the intended stunt. Leaping up and wobbling in balance on the frame, it dropped outside and disappeared once more to leave them alone.

Amber looked saddened by the animal's exit, but she expected the cat to return in its own time. The two of them sat in silence until their boredom made them fidget and somehow feed off each other's inactivity. Peter cracked first, standing up to begin a more thorough search of the house for something to do. Again he arrived at an assumption about the woman who lived there; she must have catered for having kids visiting her occasionally. Perhaps she was an aunt and saw something in a charity shop one day to keep by for when nieces or nephews visited, but the faded and yellowed cardboard of the box made him smile.

He took it back and sat on the carpet between the settees, smiling at Amber as she watched what he had in his hands expectantly. He lifted off the lid, feeling that sticky dryness where old sellotape had yellowed more than the once-white cardboard beneath. He shook the box lightly, pouring out the stiff pieces of the game and arranging them on the carpet, where Amber slid down from her seat to join him.

They played in silence, after Amber had shown Peter how to play the game using a simple demonstration. The girl had still not spoken a word since the previous night, and Peter had given up trying to get her to talk, assuming that she would speak to him in her own time if and when she was ready. They played the game, filling their plates with the good food and rejecting the bad as they made each other laugh quietly by pulling disgusted comedy faces at the worms and mud on the cards they picked.

"Aww, tummy ache," Amber said softly when she had collected a full plate of bad food. The sound made Peter jump, and he chose then to ask her what had happened.

"Was that your mum?" he asked her, "the woman with you in the other house?"

Her face dropped, and her eyes glazed over instantly. She nodded slowly then began to cry. Tears ran from both eyes and her bottom lip quivered uncontrollably. Peter leaned over to her and put a hand on the carpet beside her. She put her own hand on the top of his as he spoke.

"Don't cry," he told her, "I'll look after you."

He kept his hand there, leaning awkwardly forwards until she decided to break the contact. Just then, they both snapped their heads towards the kitchen as a half-familiar sound erupted there. The cat dragged itself back inside the open window and dropped down to trot over to the scene without recognising the important emotions on display. With its tail held vertically, it stepped lightly between them and nuzzled Amber's face and began to purr again.

———

"Sir," Johnson said in simple greeting as Captain Palmer nodded to him from the map he was hunched over. He had been summoned to assist in mission planning and walked in at the same time as Lieutenant Lloyd, who had his sleeves rolled up and his green beret worn proudly.

"Gentlemen," Palmer said to the assembled men, including three of the four navy pilots, "good morning. As you know, the powers that be are planning to send us some more assets and supplies." He held up a hand to stem the flow of questions from three of the men.

"I know, we have our priorities and they have theirs," Palmer said to change the subject away from the circuitous conversations they had already had, "They are going to give us a CO," he said with an uncommon touch of annoyance creeping into his voice, "and his own admin team, as well as some other military assets which they have been very tight-lipped regarding," he added, leaving the intimation clear in the room.

"Sneaky-beaky stuff, Sir?" Lloyd asked. His own status as leader of elite infantry would be knocked down the ladder should someone more elite be ordered to their island.

"Your guess is as good as mine, Lieutenant," Palmer said, "but that isn't the priority for today. If we are sent any specialist troops, I doubt they would fall under our domain anyway. For now, we are tasked with planning and executing a mission some sixty miles inland to escort an engineering team to and from a target."

Looks were exchanged but everyone kept quiet to wait for the rest of the information.

"You may have noticed, gentlemen," Palmer went on, "that, as disciplined as we are being, our lights are still on." He looked around the room to see the admission on their faces that they hadn't considered that fact so often taken for granted. To keep from attracting any unwelcome and cannibalistic attention, they had been operating good light discipline and only using lights that couldn't be seen from the outside. That prompted the central switch for the streetlamps on the island to be switched permanently off, and this led them to live their lives mostly in the dark anyway, so the lights remaining off wasn't that noticeable.

"That is courtesy of a nuclear power station, and yes, you guessed it, sixty miles inland," Palmer finished.

"Where's the engineering team coming from?" Lieutenant Commander Barrett asked.

"America," Palmer answered simply.

Lieutenant James Morris, Barrett's co-pilot smiled and affected a Brit's attempt at a southern states accent and said, "Now, wwhhut can they teach us about our own power station?"

"A good deal, I should imagine," piped up a nasal voice from behind the navy pilots as Second Lieutenant Palmer walked in to hand a sheet of paper to his older brother, "seeing as they designed and built it for us about ten years ago."

Johnson's eyebrows lowered slightly as he fought against the natural urge to narrow his eyes in suspicion that the most junior officer was in possession of information that the others had not yet been given. The balance of power was tentative, although the officer classes were too polite to mention the vulgarity of who should be in charge, as the navy pilots were army equivalent ranks of majors and captains themselves. Command of ground activities, however, had been devolved to Palmer as the most qualified. For all the men present, all of them were very aware that the Captain's younger brother was tolerated under sufferance only due to his older brother, just so long as he didn't get in the way of anything. For him to swan into a senior officers' meeting and act as he did set every spine in the room firmly on edge.

"Thank you, Second Lieutenant," Captain Palmer said with a chilly tone of official annoyance, then scowled gently at his brother's back as he left the room. He was too well bred to offer an apology for his sibling's words, so he continued to explain.

"The yanks have sent a carrier," he said, his expression meaning nothing derogatory as he clearly had an affinity with the Americans after working with them in Germany, "and they've apparently pre-empted our nuclear needs. They built two for us, and they believe that both of them will be at risk of overheating or some such problem in the near future. We need to get them there safely, clear out the place, then keep them safe until they can stabilise the reactors and do some kind of witchcraft with cooling."

Lieutenant Commander Murray whistled low, looking to his naval colleagues, who seemed to understand. He saw the two army men looking at them expectantly and explained.

"If the Americans have sent a carrier, that must mean they've sent an entire carrier strike group," he said, seeing that this news still hadn't sunk in.

"That means a carrier," he said as he checked off on one finger, "at least one destroyer, a pair of frigates, half a dozen support ships and," he glanced at the other pilots, "a nuclear attack sub."

Then it sunk in, and their faces showed fresh nervousness.

"Any word from the Soviets?" Johnson asked in an uncharacteristically taut voice.

"Nothing," Palmer said with equable seriousness, "and nothing from the Chinese either. It appears that Communism doesn't want to speak to Democracy, even when hell empties and all the devils are here."

Palmer's lapse into Shakespearean prose betrayed just how much time he had spent glued to the planning board and the radio. He was tired, not just physically but emotionally, and his own personal war was being swallowed by the global politics in play. Everyone around the table understood the potential severity of the response that the Soviet Union could feel forced into. Even though the Cold War was, as they all believed, in its dying stages and intelligence reported that the Union was close to collapse, none of them could even begin to predict what a desperate government would do, given the current climate, if they felt threatened. The arrival of a carrier strike group and an American nuclear attack submarine only a few hundred miles away in the English Channel ran the obvious risk of disaster.

"Why haven't we spoken to them yet?" Lieutenant Lloyd asked the room rhetorically, "Surely they can see that what's going on is bigger than countries fighting each other?"

"One would have hoped so, but that is somewhat beyond our control for now," Palmer answered to move the conversation onwards, "Now, they should be here by tonight, I'm assured, rendezvous with the joint fleet in the Channel, and will send their men in tomorrow morning to us. I assume via helicopter, even though the means haven't been confirmed to us as yet. I can only presume that we might be expecting our new commanding officer and his entourage at that time, so I would fully anticipate being evicted from here. Whatever other personnel come with them, if any, will be our responsibility to house and feed but I highly doubt they will become our men to instruct. So," he paused, "assuming the mission will go ahead, I propose that I lead it via one of the Sultan wagons," he said as he kept his eyes down and away from Johnson's, "I'm sure we can all agree that taking my Chieftain would be slow going and possibly be a touch of overkill, but I want a troop of the Fox cars with me and one quarter of your marines," he added, looking up to Lloyd and receiving a nod, "Your sergeant will suffice, and I presume we can spare a man to drive them in a Saxon?" he asked, finally making eye contact with Johnson, who was just waiting to be told he was sitting that one out. He nodded, going over the particulars, which mainly encompassed routes and alternatives, and left the actual entry, assault and clearance of the power plant as general intentions rather than specific actions, as the men coming from America knew the plant intimately and would be needed to make those calls.

"If I may, Sir?" Johnson asked politely, having calmed

down from his initial annoyance of not being allowed out to play. Palmer gestured for him to speak.

"I'd suggest splitting your marines over two Saxons, with an engineer in each," he said simply, leaving the obvious reasons out of his explanation.

"Very good, Sarn't Major," the captain answered with a nod as he saw the logic in the recommendation instantly, "tomorrow then, we should know more when they arrive, but I'd like men ready and briefed. Thank you."

Johnson left, trying to decide whether to throw Sergeant Strauss back into the lion's den or to put trust in others he wasn't totally certain of.

FOURTEEN

Pauline finished her allocated work duty of cooking and cleaning in the hotel's modest kitchens. There were over thirty people there now, half of whom would leave if they could guarantee success in finding somewhere safer to be. It was the lesser of two evils. When she returned, she found Ellie in the same position; sitting on the bed with her heels tight into her thighs and her forehead rested on her knees. She didn't look up when Pauline was shown back into the room, not even when she placed a wrapped meal of fresh bread sandwiches in front of her.

Pauline went into the bathroom of their hotel room-cum-cell, and when she came back out, she saw Ellie eating the food with her cheeks puffed out and her jaw working almost desperately as she raised the fingertips of one hand to her lips.

"Sorry," she said through her full mouth, "I just…"

"Don't be silly, my lovely," Pauline told her kindly as she sat down opposite her, "I brought it back for you anyway, you need to get your strength up."

Ellie chewed and winced as she swallowed her mouthful too soon and had to force the lump down her throat.

"The bread," she gasped before snatching another bite, "where did it come from?"

"I made it," Pauline said simply, "the kitchens here still work fine, and all I have to do is make food. They don't make me do anything else," she went on, pausing hesitantly before continuing and speaking faster to change the subject, "and they keep the people out, so it's a fair enough trade…"

Ellie looked at her seriously with dark, red-rimmed eyes.

"You think it's fair?" she asked dangerously, "They snatch people away from their families and you think it's fair?"

"No," Pauline said carefully, dropping her own smile, "I don't think what they've done is fair at all, but I don't know what I'd be doing if they hadn't come here. I'm just trying to get by, and I don't think I can… I don't think I can kill people."

"Well I'm bloody ready to," Ellie responded. Eager to change the subject, Pauline pointed at the battered paperback book on the low bedside table beside her.

"Did you read any of that?" she asked, hopeful that she had been given a lover of literature to share a room with.

"No," Ellie answered through another mouthful of food, "I haven't got my glasses and I can't hold it far enough away to see it."

Her words were full of regret and annoyance, but any response Pauline could make was stopped by the knock at the door.

The two women looked at each other before Ellie shrugged, and Pauline shouted for whoever it was to come in.

One of the first men to turn up there stood in the doorway, not stepping inside, and politely asked for Ellie to come with him.

"Why?" she shot back, full of venom.

"Because our Boss would like to talk to you," he responded.

Pauline expected more anger, more revolt and even imagined them having to drag the woman out of the room, but Ellie simply stood, brushed off the crumbs from her dirty and stained clothes, and followed him.

Ellie walked tall, pride and anger keeping her from unravelling. She was shown to the door of the big hall in the historical building and the man who had escorted her there gestured for her to go inside. That was evidently as far as he was taking her.

She walked in, looking around at the high ceilings and decorated walls, and a voice cut through to her.

"Good afternoon," came a man's voice from her right. She looked to see a man of average height and build, with an unremarkable face. His voice had nothing unique about it either, but there was something intangible about the man that made him appear strong. He didn't ooze malevolence or physically dominate her; in fact, he kept a respectful distance as he spoke.

"I owe you an apology," he said, "but I know a simple apology won't help you at all. Believe me when I say that I know the loss you feel right now…" He gestured to an ornate chair beside one that he took, inviting her to sit with him. She sat, her face a mask of neutrality.

"I want you to know that I sent men back to where you were and had them search until they were forced to come back, but they found no sign of her. My own daughter was lost very early on," he said with eyes turned down, "even before most people realised what was happening. We'd been visiting family near Portsmouth and, well, I don't need to tell you…"

"I'm very sorry," Ellie said, seeing him look up to smile at her. That smile faded when her face contorted, and she spoke again.

"But *your* daughter wasn't left for dead by thugs who knocked her mother out. *Your* daughter didn't die alone and terrified. *My* daughter did. She's dead because of you," she finished, spitting the words at him with a jab of her right index finger. When she had finished, her body betrayed her and brought on angry tears caused by adrenaline, and it opened the floodgates once more.

The man sat back and just watched her cry. He didn't force his words on her, didn't tell her that the men were simply being clumsy and ham-fisted about following his orders to bring back survivors to the safety of their hill. They had never encountered anyone who didn't want to be rescued, so the thought never occurred to them that people might want to be left alone. He wanted to say that he would have done things differently, that he would have brought the girl back with them and listened to her, but felt the words were empty so he didn't say them.

He also didn't tell her that his men had found a dead zombie in the house, which he doubted a little girl could have achieved. He didn't tell her that he believed someone had found her before his men had got back to them. She appeared to have decided and accepted that the girl was gone, so he saw no need to drive her insane with renewed hopes and fears, deciding that it was better to let her accept the loss and move on.

"I know there's nothing I can say to make this better," he told her, "but you have my word that nothing like this will happen again."

"You're right," she sniffed, "nothing you can say will help."

With that, she stood and walked from the room with steps that gathered pace until she broke into a run just before the doorway.

The man, John Michaels, leaned back in the chair and sighed. He longed for men who had the intelligence to follow orders but reminded himself that he had to adapt and work with what he had. The tale about his daughter was true, but he left out some pertinent facts.

Facts such as his daughter turning in the car as he sped home, his wife in the back seat holding her as she convulsed with the fever. He left out that the girl had opened her eyes suddenly and bitten her mother hard, tearing out a golf ball-sized chunk from her neck and sheeting the inside of the car with arterial spray from her torn blood vessels. He didn't tell her that he had crashed the car in his sudden and terrifying blindness, and that his unrestrained daughter had flown through the windscreen on impact to roll to a bloody and broken mess thirty feet from the wreck. He didn't tell her that when he came around from the blow to his head, that his wife was reaching for him but unable to do more than hook a single fingernail into his clothing and try to pull him towards her milky eyes and gnashing teeth. He didn't say that he fell from his car in terror, scrambling backwards on his backside to put distance between himself and the horror. He didn't say that the horror only grew infinitely worse when a crackling, gargling sound came from the ground behind him and he turned to see his daughter dragging her shattered and twisted frame towards him an inch at a time, as though sheer determination and hunger could force her ruined body to move.

He was ashamed of himself for what he did afterwards, and when he went back over a week later with the resolve to end their perpetual suffering, he found his daughter had moved close to a mile away from where she had last reached out to him. Her minute progress had been unceasing as she followed the direction that her last meal had gone in. He dispatched her, freed her from her useless body, with a single shot to the back of her head from the Browning semi-automatic he had removed from the armoury. He used the same method to kill his wife, shooting her in the temple through the back wind-screen of the car as she turned to try and locate the source of the sound. He left their bodies where they were, no longer considering them to have been the people he loved and satis-fied himself that whatever part of them that was left had been set free.

He returned to where he had parked the van he was using and drove back to the place they had fortified, having narrowly avoided being swept away by the massive horde that had inexplicably gathered and stormed across the countryside, leaving filth and destruction in their wake. He used the van because the other vehicle he had scavenged was a little too high profile for everyday use.

He couldn't explain why he hadn't reported to the camp, not that he had been home to receive the call anyway, and instead, he'd watched it until it was empty and sneaked in to steal weapons and the Warrior tank. He didn't know why he felt it necessary to abandon his duties, especially seeing as the army was the only family he had left, and the men of his Sabre troop would have been his responsibility as much as his daughter had been.

He decided that he'd had enough of being part of the machine, as he illogically blamed that machine and its masters for his family dying. Instead he drank until he was sick, drank again, and dreamt up a new way of life.

FIFTEEN

The alarm went up shortly before three in the morning.

The alarm, such as it was, was the massively loud mechanical, metallic chattering of the coaxial machine gun on the turret of the Chieftain tank blocking the road. The radio sparked to life, fire support was requested, and the standby troops poured from their billets to form up at the threshold between the island and the bridge.

The direction of the enemy was given, and the two Fox cars stationed permanently on the two bluffs of higher ground erupted into life as they added their own bursts of automatic fire to the fray.

Sergeant Horton, taking his turn to sleep in the tank with all but the commander's hatch down to preserve their heat in the dead of night, was woken by the two members of his crew who were awake and taking turns to look through their handheld optics to stare at the empty roadway. Only at that time it suddenly wasn't empty.

The thin tripwire rigged at the far end activated the flares attached to the bridge with an echoing pop to bathe the area in a soft glow.

The reticuled display hazed into a grainy collection of shapes as a stumbling, shuffling group of zombies materialised, making the man babble a string of incoherent noises in surprise before he got his brain into gear and snatched up the controls of the weapon to stitch a burst of 7.62 into them.

The two sleeping men, one being the tank's commander, leapt instantly to life and in seconds, the second machine gun on the tank rattled out its own shots.

Horton looked through the optics, snatched up the radio and called the two Fox cars. Within thirty seconds, their two guns added a devastating additional weight and the impetus of the advance had been halted. The optics flared brightly as the standby force behind them had set up and fired a 51mm illuminating mortar round, which sank slowly through the air behind the onslaught, showing it to number well over a hundred.

With four guns firing on them, the slow-moving infantry of the dead found their attack 'rendered safe' in less than a minute, but that didn't mean the island defenders were out of the woods straightaway.

As the guns stopped when no further targets remained standing, Captain Palmer emerged wearing his camouflaged trousers and boots, with a white PT shirt under his webbing that was still unfastened. He had a Browning pistol in the holster on his belt, his Sterling sub-machine gun in his hands with the bayonet already fixed in place. The man must have woken, dressed and been ready to fight inside of thirty seconds to make it to the bridge before the firing had fully stopped. Directly behind him came Lieutenant Lloyd, similarly dressed and equally ready to bring the fight to their enemy.

"Five of yours, five of mine?" he asked Lloyd, who nodded and shouted five names into the night to have his marines come to him. Palmer turned to look at the men of the Yeomanry, picking out the first five men that he knew by name. The twelve men stepped up, fixed bayonets and readied themselves, as Palmer turned to the men of Maxwell's assault troop who had set up their mortar.

"Hold, just stand by with an illumination round," he told them, not waiting for a response but turning back to his assembled team, "bayonets, unless you see obvious bullet wounds to the head, then you make damn sure before you step close to them. One in the head, dump them off the road and stay close to each other."

They waited, staring off into the dark past the tank that they trusted, to keep their night optics trained on the approach. After an hour and a half, the sun began to rise off to their right. In that time, others had come to check the situation, and everyone not directly needed was sent away. They didn't go far, and one of the men even returned to the officer's quarters and fetched Palmer's uniform smock for him. When the sun had risen enough, he turned to his team and addressed them.

"Ready?"

They were.

"Let's go," he said, calling up to the now-open hatches of the tank to give the order to cease fire. Horton confirmed the order with a thumbs-up gesture and watched as the twelve men went to work.

Palmer spread them out in a line, calling for a slow approach to the first of them which lay face down. The back of its skull was missing, indicating that the body posed no risk to them by then. It, she, was kicked off the side of the roadway to drop and splash into the water below. They moved carefully, never taking chances with the unmoving ones, and making sure with those still squirming with whatever intact body parts they still possessed. None of them was fast moving enough to make the soldiers fire a shot, and the only burst of adrenaline came from the time when a knot of them had fallen on top of a smaller one who was freed after the weight fell away.

A smaller one, that was a better way to say it.

Having rendered safe a smaller one was far easier to live with, made it slightly better when sleeping at night, instead of saying that they had killed a child. It went down to the bayonet of a marine with the slightly longer reach of his rifle and was sent over the edge with the others in uncomfortable silence.

The sun was fully up when their exhausted group filed back through the small gap made by the tank, and just then the sky above the sea filled with the sound of helicopters.

Rushing back over the bridge, the twelve men were subjected to a rapid body search to establish no wounds, then allowed to carry on into the island as per their revised standing orders.

SIXTEEN

Shortly after dawn the island, or at least those not already woken by the earlier gunfire, was woken by the shatteringly-loud noise of helicopters swooping in and hovering to land. Johnson, expecting the early morning arrivals as he was privy to the information, was alarmed as many others were from where they toiled near the bridge. He craned his neck up towards the higher ground where the only flat, open space large enough to accommodate the aircraft lay. He allowed himself a crooked smile as he watched the two recognisable silhouettes of a pair of Sea Kings dropping in. The other silhouette was unique, and made his mouth hang open slightly. The aircraft had been escorted by another helicopter that hovered high over the island in overwatch. An Apache, with its stubby wings sprouting pods of rockets, loomed almost malevo-lently in the air as the two transport helicopters disgorged their contents.

As the two aircraft rose to take off only thirty seconds after landing, with their engine notes dialling up intensity, another helicopter flew in from the direction of the sea, only this time it was the profile of a Bell. Johnson wasn't knowledgeable enough to tell who it belonged to but had to guess that it was American. That helicopter flew directly over them heading inland, and when the Sea Kings had turned their noses back out to sea to fly away, the Apache moved from its unnervingly steady hover, dipped its own nose, and followed the Bell.

Frowning, Johnson walked towards the headquarters building and prepared for the influx of experts.

The Bedford truck that had been coaxed up the steep roads in anticipation of bringing down their new guests returned to the lower slopes shortly after the air had returned to still silence. The canvas flap at the back was in its normal position of up, and a small unit of camouflaged uniformed soldiers hopped down and retrieved various heavy kit bags and weapons.

The last man down, crisply uniformed and moustached, with thickly-rimmed glasses between moustache and beret, strode to Johnson and waited for a salute.

The SSM's eyes ran over the insignia, the crowned rose, and the crowns on the shoulders.

"Sir," he said as he drew himself up to attention and saluted briefly.

"Squadron Sergeant Major Johnson, I presume?" said the man as he returned the salute in acknowledgment.

"Yessir."

"Major Hadlington," he said smoothly before unnecessarily adding, "Intelligence Corps."

Johnson had known in less than a heartbeat that the man was a major, and that he was Green Slime through and through from the insignia and the look of him. Johnson, like just about every member of Her Majesty's Armed Forces employed in a combat arm, had a deep mistrust of the intelligence corps and often made the common jest about 'army intelligence' being the world's biggest oxymoron. The corps had only recently been bumped up from being a support arm into a combat support arm, and although the difference sounded small, it served to elevate the men and women of the intelligence corps from rear-echelon to something closer to the sharp end of the spear, in their eyes.

He knew that elevation was due to the work they had evolved into 'over the water' and he had met a few of them who were part of something known simply as 'the detachment', which was their elite counter-terrorist surveillance unit. The men, and women, he reminded himself, of those units were respected and revered in certain circles, because they put their lives on the line just as the troops on the ground did.

The one thing that Johnson was wrong about, was his guess that the moustached major would have a double-barrelled name. He was expecting something utterly Etonian like the Simpkins-Palmer boys he had to endure, then felt a stab of guilt for thinking that, as only one of those men was a useless fop of an aristocrat, in his book.

Major Raymond Hadlington, while in possession of the breeding and accent associated with the mockery of the enlisted ranks, was a hard-working man who demanded precision and efficiency from those under his command. He felt that he had the right to demand this, as he led by example. His team, some of whom he had worked with previously, had been working effectively from their cramped quarters on board the Royal Navy frigate.

Their panicked flight from their base in Germany two weeks previously, as the fence line was swarmed by a flowing, roiling mass of corpses, was still fresh in their collective minds. As was the helicopter ride that evacuated them minutes before the fence collapsed and the dead poured inside.

That desperate escape was another story, and not one that Hadlington wanted to remember, because to him it signalled that the army had abandoned the continent that held the majority of their forces.

Being a major in the intelligence arena, he was far from the mushroom status of most force personnel, who claimed to be kept permanently in the dark and fed bullshit. He knew that continental Europe was all but gone, and he knew that the Soviets were unleashing hell on the eastern borders to stop the flow of infected bodies walking over the expanse of land borders, with flight after flight of bombers laying waste to the hordes.

To the west, the Americans stopped all traffic heading in their direction, and ran near constant aerial surveillance by using two of their AWACS, refuelled in mid-air with as many personnel on board as they could manage. The drain on that constant air surveillance had been alleviated with the arrival of the US carrier fleet. Hadlington was also hearing rumours that forces were being dispatched to Iceland, and they had even struck some kind of deal with the remaining Spanish government surviving on their cluster of islands off the western coast of Africa to begin sending vessels and aircraft. Seeing as the islands had shut their borders entirely, allowing the US forces to take over the airports in exchange for the promise of financial reparations was an easy decision for them to make.

In other parts of the world they were preparing to strengthen their own defences and effectively hunker down until the terrifying mess sorted itself out.

When Major Hadlington was told he would be returning to the UK, he was confused at first, then he was informed of the pockets of resistance which were mainly military-led. He was given the information regarding the UK's strength, then tasked with taking a team to conduct operations on the south coast for the newly-formed joint command at sea group. He was given the personnel list, assembled them and brought them all up to speed on the global situation and then laid out his own personal rules for how they would operate as a unit.

Now as he strode confidently into the low, dark building

that purported to be the island's headquarters, he wrinkled his nose at the stale air and ordered the windows opened to purge it. He walked over to the radio operator, Corporal Daniels, and cleared his throat.

"Stand by one," Daniels said into the mic before standing and offering a salute, "Daniels, Sir," he introduced himself, then waited to be given permission to resume his duties.

Hadlington kept him waiting on his feet, before turning to look at his own personnel.

"Ward?" he said, and a female corporal stepped towards them, "Take over from Daniels here, make sure you get a full disposition before you relieve him."

"Sir," she acknowledged, turning to look at Daniels expectantly.

"And Corporal," Hadlington said over his shoulder, "there will be no smoking inside this control room from now on, in case you are recalled to duty here."

Daniels looked at his replacement, who stared at him blankly. Feeling awkward and admonished as his comfortably dark and smoky surroundings were transformed, he put the cigarette out in the cold remains of his coffee cup and sat back down to hand over his station.

Hadlington spread a new map over the central table, showing the target location in finer detail. He had been told that the armoured unit was on standby to move out and waited for their commanding officer to report to him.

After five minutes he had not appeared, so he called for a runner. A Lance Corporal arrived before him, and he sent the man, or the boy more like, away with curt instructions.

"Ward, any update from Charlie-One-One yet?" he asked the new radio operator, who was tidying the workstation, wearing a look of distaste.

"Stand by, Sir," she said, then reached for the set to turn dials and transmit using her clear radio voice.

"Charlie-One-One, this is Zero, Charlie-One-One, Zero, over," she said almost robotically.

A pause extended to almost ten seconds before she repeated the line using the exact same precise intonations and rhythm for each word.

"Nothing, Sir," she said after her second attempt, "stand by,"

"Jeeves-Five-Three, Jeeves-Five-Three, come in," she said, visibly grimacing at the vulgarity she suspected would follow.

"Jeeves-Five-Three, receiving," came the static reply from the speaker in what neither of them recognised as a Virginia accent. The background noise behind the words was a screaming, chattering whine.

"Five-Three," Ward said, refusing to use the American aviator's callsign, which she suspected had been chosen specifically to annoy the British, "update on Charlie-One-One progress?"

"Your boys are on the ground as of six minutes ago, Jeeves is *en-route*," both Ward and Hadlington winced at his pronunciation of the terminology, "to the next objective and the cab is RTB."

The lead pilot in the Apache signed off from the Brits and smirked a small smile of satisfaction to himself, because he had annoyed the female operator into not using the callsign he had picked intentionally for the purpose of pissing off his allies. Cruising along at a steady four hundred feet and one hundred and sixty miles per hour, the ground below him sped by in a blur. He saw occasional snippets of detail if he glanced down, but each time he did so he usually saw something he didn't want to remember. Blasting over the low, rolling lush green of the countryside in between small pockets of habitation, he saw those snippets now. A white car sitting at an unnatural angle with its nose in a ditch. A small knot of people standing around aimlessly and staring upwards at the same time in response to the sound of his engines, a building, blackened by fire and almost entirely without a roof, then a sight that upset him.

Two kids, one small and one smaller, carrying bags and walking in the middle of a single lane road with hedgerows on each side, wandering aimlessly, or so it seemed.

Hadlington, as offended as his very British sensibilities were, straightened and nodded. He now knew that the ground team, Charlie-One-One, who he knew only as a four-man team that he hadn't met, which spoke volumes as to their identity, was now at the objective. The annoying Apache pilot was currently flying east towards the gathering swarm outside north London for their own mission, and the 'cab' being the approximation of Charlie-One-One's taxi, was returning to its base out on the English Channel. They would not see either aircraft again.

Hadlington knew that he had seniors and counterparts in other places, mostly still on the gathering flotilla of giant crew ships in the Channel, which were a mixture of British, French, American and Norwegian. He knew that there were other Charlie teams out there from the allocation of callsigns alone and wondered what their objectives were.

The door opened, and his ponderings ceased as he turned to face a smiling young Captain with the red eyes of a man who had probably drunk to excess the previous night and who had yet to shave that morning. He sketched a salute without waiting for it to be acknowledged and held out his hand.

"Julian Simpkins-Palmer, Household Cavalry," he said introducing himself.

"Hadlington, Intelligence," he responded brusquely as he shook the offered hand.

Palmer learned everything he needed to from that simple exchange.

Hadlington, he guessed, was a man without humour who had no time in his busy schedule for human interaction that didn't directly involve something tangible and achievable. He probably made an instant judgement about the Captain from both his age and his appearance, but Palmer was not so insecure as to offer an explanation or an apology. He reckoned that Hadlington would probably disapprove of his spending time with the men under his command and mucking in with the dirty work when the timing was right. He would probably think that Palmer's internal database of the men's first names as well as their surnames was an ineffective waste of time for an officer, along with the few personal details he tried to recall for any man under his command.

He felt as though he had failed himself when trooper Harris died, because he didn't know his first name. He only recalled that he wasn't originally from the area but had moved because his father was in the navy, and that his signing up to the army had caused a family disagreement which he guessed would never be resolved now.

The major hadn't even abbreviated his unit to the accepted 'Int Corps' that was the norm, and Palmer didn't even want to consider his opinion on the capabilities of the men, given that they were predominantly reservists and not full-time soldiers.

"Captain," Hadlington said, "I was informed that your men were equipped and ready to move. Is that not the case?"

"It is, Sir," he said, "and they are. We had a spot of bother in the night is all."

"Bother?" Hadlington asked, taken aback.

"Yes, Sir, seems a few of the blighters got wind of us here and made a concerted effort to come in uninvited. Been at it since about four this morning clearing them out and only just finished. If that's all for now, Sir? I'd like to get cleaned up if you don't mind?"

"Yes, of course," Hadlington answered, a little shocked.

Just then, the Bedford returned from its second journey to

the top of the hill to squeak to a loud halt outside the building just as Johnson greeted Palmer.

"The usual slime," Johnson opined about the unsmiling major.

"Now, now, Mister Johnson," he admonished the man gently with a smile of his own, "but I don't think we will have a problem getting around him."

Johnson opened his mouth to agree, to offer his opinion on being under orders of a Major who would suffer the runaround from the troops, but at that moment their problems were compounded.

The last man to climb down from the bed of the truck among his personal entourage wore the uniform of the Royal Scots. He had two privates in the same uniform caps attending him as his bag men and, as though some portent of imminent bad luck, wore the two stars and a crown of a full Colonel.

Both Palmer and Johnson deflated as one, the latter even letting a small groan of disappointment escape his lips. The Colonel noticed them at that point and stepped towards them beaming a smile. He walked with a curious gait, looking to pause on the ball of each foot before lifting the limb quickly, as though to catch up and make good the time lost from the hesitation. His face seemed genuinely happy to see them, but had an air of falsehood to it, as though he were on display for the film crews in some backwater country, giving out fake smiles to support the foreign interests of UK PLC.

"Colonel Tim Munro, Royal Scots," he introduced himself with the same broad smile and no hint of a Scottish accent. Both men swelled to attention and offered salutes; Johnson with his right hand to his eyebrow and Palmer with his submachine gun held vertically in his left hand against his body and performing his salute with his right hand held against the weapon.

"At ease, chaps," he said, "and you are?"

"Captain Palmer, Sir, Household Cavalry."

Colonel Tim nodded affably and muttered, "Splendid, splendid," then looked expectantly to Johnson.

"Squadron Sergeant Major Johnson, Sir," he said woodenly, "C Squadron Yeomanry."

"Splendid," Colonel Tim said again, then seemed to grow bored with their company and turned away only to swing back and offer a mutter of advice to Palmer.

"Captain, perhaps you'd prefer to shave and change before we meet again? Show a better example for the men, eh? Good lad."

"Yes Sir," Palmer said, "sorry, Sir, won't happen again."

The two men sank again as the kindly old fool walked away.

"Well, bugger me," Palmer said in a low breath as his hands ran over the scratchy stubble on his chin.

"Rather not, Sir," Johnson said automatically, "but I suspect we've just crapped in our own mess tin getting that shower of shit land on us."

"Mess *Tim,*" Palmer responded drily.

And the two of them finally realised the double blow their command structure had just dealt them. The intelligence corps major was too junior to be a wrinkle to the army personnel, let alone the Royal Marines, but the combination of the meticulous major and the blustering buffoon of a full Colonel was a true *fait accompli;* one made the suggestions but the other gave the orders. The major could be circumvented, given his status with the men and the Colonel could be 'handled' but the combination of them rendered the forces on the ground powerless.

Palmer, as exhausted as he was, led the seven vehicles of his expedition across the road bridge within an hour of the arrival of their new commanding officer and his staff. He took Two Troop under the command of Sergeant Rod Sinclair. Johnson had flatly refused to allow Maxwell's assault troop to go for two reasons; firstly, that their Spartans needed maintenance, and secondly that Maxwell had been in the vanguard of almost every mission they had run since the whole lunacy began. For a similar reason he left Strauss' troop off the menu, as they hadn't had a chance to fully recover from losing a man on their last venture outside the safety of the island. That left his two other Sabre troops, and of those, Sinclair's was deemed the steadiest. Three Troop was a mixture of troopers moulded into one team of twelve that hadn't yet obtained that kind of fighting unit cohesion they needed, at least not in Johnson's opinion anyway, and that was what mattered.

He had relented and borrowed a reliable man from both Maxwell's and Strauss' troops to drive the two Saxons and taxi the eight Royal Marines under the leadership of their sergeant, Bill Hampton. In each of those armoured personnel carriers were four marines and a single nuclear engineer from America. The suggestion to split the precious cargo was a sensible precaution, as each of the skilled men was effectively protected by his own 'brick', or four-man patrol. Sticking to that template made it more likely that at least one of them would remain unharmed and capable of preventing the power station going boom.

The last vehicle, sitting in the middle between the Saxons with two Foxes fore and aft, was the Sultan vehicle that Johnson wished he had been in. He had lent him his radio operator, Corporal Daniels, as the man had been left looking for work after his ejection from the headquarters building.

Johnson watched them out of sight, not knowing that they would face nothing of the resistance they expected.

SEVENTEEN

Major Clive Downes stayed on one knee and looked over the iron sights and fat, suppressed barrel of the brand new MP5SD he had been issued along with his men. They were all familiar with the weapons, having used them extensively when their squadron rotated onto the 'Black' team, but the sudden change felt slightly alien.

They had just spent seven months living in the caves and villages with the Mujahedeen, as unsavoury as the experience was, and had been carrying the plentiful AK47s that flooded half of the world. There was no need for heavy calibre penetration with this strange new enemy, and their distance needs were catered for by one of his men who carried the rarest of possessions in the western military; that of the Soviet VAL 9mm silenced sniper rifle.

That weapon had been one of the reasons that US and UK special forces had been in Afghanistan, as the Soviet technological advances with an active war for testing, had been astronomical. Consequently, samples of new weapons were highly sought after to enable them to produce effective countermeasures, should the Cold War turn hot. That captured rifle had never made it into the hands of the civilian masters, however, and would now be employed against the dead instead of being rigorously tested and reverse-engineered.

The arms race had become the new space race, with each side of the globe working tirelessly to develop new weaponry to beat the defences of their potential opposition.

With their rapid-firing suppressed machine guns and their silenced sniper rifle, their doomsday options were strapped to the backs of two of them in the forms of shotguns; fully automatic shotguns, for when they had no option but to go loud.

Their sidearms, as with many special forces teams, were a mixture as they had access to a choice of weapons to suit their individual preferences. The regular troops, what the men of the Special Air Service referred to as the Green Army, would never be allowed to pick their weapons or show individual flavours as they did. Two of them carried the Browning Hi-Power, one carried the American Colt .45 and their Major preferred the Sig-Sauer P228.

Those four men, with their weapon-based idiosyncrasies, possessed enough firepower and lethal training to perform as an entire platoon of regular soldiers. Now, kneeling in a rough circle facing outwards, they listened as the sounds of the helicopter blades faded away into silence.

As if the four men had evolved to become streamlined instruments of warfare, even their names were mostly single-syllable. Their officer, nominally in charge but in their arena at the peak of their chosen profession every man had a say, was known simply as Boss or The Boss to the men. The men, a corporal and two troopers, were similarly named Mac, Desmond or 'Dezzy' and Smiffy. He introduced himself as Smiffy with two fs, in his cheeky south London accent. Desmond wasn't Dezzy's real name, but it was a joke at his expense from his parent unit, who said they would see him soon and dubbed him Desmond Tutu, as in Two-Two for 22

SAS, when he left for Hereford on selection. The joke back-
fired, as he passed selection on his first attempt and retained
the nickname in celebration.

To outsiders, their curious tight-knit nature seemed unnatural and very un-army-like. But outsiders didn't understand
them. Other than their Major, who retained his rank when
passing selection, when ordinarily he would have been forced
to rotate out after two or three years, as he had done when he'd
served his first stint in the regiment as a captain. The enlisted
men lost whatever rank they held in their parent units and
often went from sergeants or corporals back to being troopers.
The fact that the major had been invited back for a second
stint spoke volumes about his competency.

The sound of rotor blades faded into silence and Mac's soft
Scottish voice drifted to the others from behind them as they
covered their own sectors of fire.

"Three, slow movers, one hundred yards," he muttered.

"Smiffy," the major said, "on you."

Trooper Smith said nothing but turned and lay flat,
pointing towards the direction Mac was facing. He slipped the
long rifle from his shoulder and settled into the stock, pausing
a few heartbeats before the three whistling coughs barked
from the gun. All three zombies fell, and the Major called the
move.

They stepped towards the big power plant in bounds; two
men covering and two men moving. The main access door was
opened with a swipe card which had been coded and provided
by their colonial cousins. The door opened with a tiny metallic
buzz and Mac held the handle of the door as he glanced back
to see the other three stacked up in tight formation with their
MP5s up and ready.

They went in, clearing the building section by section and
finding only a dozen people inside the compound after three
hours of thorough searching. Not people specifically, but

undead, lurching creatures who had been, up until fairly recently, people.

"Call it in," Downes said to Mac, who was carrying their radio, and watched as he snaked out the antenna on the ground.

"Zero, this is Charlie-One-One. Zero, Charlie-One-One, over," he said in low, robotic tones.

"One-One, Zero, send," came the female voice from the other end of the ether.

"One-One, target secure. ETA on convoy?"

"Stand by, one," came the operator's voice before a brief pause, "ETA one-nine minutes, over."

Mac glanced at the Boss, who nodded back. Nineteen minutes until the engineers arrived with their armoured escort to stop the plant from going critical. Mac acknowledged the information and signed off to pack up the radio gear. Nineteen minutes came and went in relative quiet, other than the two shambling callers at the gate. The four men still maintained cover and situational awareness, ingrained habits they were unable to switch off after a life of considering incoming enemy fire. They had yet to see a zombie with the ability to bring a weapon to bear, but carelessness, as Mac liked to say, often led to a mild case of death.

The two callers were allowed to come close, then both took single rounds in the skull as they coughed from Dezzy's MP5 at a distance of twenty feet. They had learned to be economical with their shots, unless faced with one of the rare faster ones that usually denoted a sizeable force of zombies would soon follow. This experience had been earned shortly after their return from the sub to the surface of the water, when told they would be employed for precision missions and would be inserted far behind enemy lines, such as they were. Downes requested a day in theatre for training, as the intelligence briefs held no mention or description of how to fight them.

The powers that be allowed the request after a day of deliberation, evidently deciding that their small team was replaceable should they not return, and the intelligence they could bring back would be worthwhile.

Given that they had already been told that sound attracted them, and that a tiny percentage of them acted differently and were more dangerous, Downes requested the suppressed MP5s. They flew by helicopter to a sparsely-populated region of northern France and spent six hours developing tactics which they reported back to command. Their rules were simple:

- small groups, low noise profile,
- use suppressed weapons whenever possible,
- avoid large concentrations of enemy and drop the faster ones at distance as soon identification made,
- then clear out before arrival of their faithful followers.

Their tactics were under the radar, invisible, and quiet. The rest of the time was waited out in silence, until the whistling and squeaking of moving armour tickled the edges of their hearing. Nobody said anything, because they didn't have to. An armoured convoy was the exact opposite of the warfare that they practised, and although impressive and able to bring a staggering and devastating amount of firepower to bear, they also attracted every shuffling corpse inside of a mile radius just by driving along the road, even before they fired a shot.

The diversionary tactic from the American Apache pilot should have helped, as he flew over fifty miles east before destroying a large road bridge to stem the flow of corpses and contain them. This also served to make a lot of noise and attract anything heading in the direction of the power station away towards the fast-flowing river and the sea beyond where the bridge had collapsed.

As the seven vehicles stormed in and had the gates pushed closed behind them, the four men jogged in to the entrance where the convoy formed a semi-circle and faced their guns outwards. A man wearing a captain's insignia stepped down from a tracked light tank and met the four men as they arrived.

"Captain Palmer," he said to the men, who weren't in the slightest bit breathless after their quarter-mile run from the gate, "Household Cavalry."

"Captain," acknowledged Mac as the first man to have arrived, giving Palmer the incorrect assumption that he was the officer leading the group. Downes stayed back from the conversation, waiting to hear what transpired.

"I presume you've been inside?" Palmer asked, guessing that the four men with wild beards and piercing eyes were clearly what his men would call *sneaky-beaky*, and probably wouldn't have felt it necessary to wait for half a squad of marines to check out an abandoned building.

"It's clear," Mac said simply, "you've brought the engineers?"

In answer, two men were escorted towards the doors, with four marines surrounding each one.

"We'll take it from here," Downes said, stepping forward and speaking for the first time. Palmer's eyebrows rose slightly, indicating that his trained ear had picked up on the educated voice and had clearly misunderstood who the officer was. Given the man's age, Palmer also correctly surmised in an eye-blink that the man was his senior and responded accordingly.

"Of course, Sir," he answered, "I shall set the perimeter and wait for instructions."

Downes nodded his thanks to him and turned to indicate that the two engineers should follow. The six men disappeared inside after the door was swiped open, leaving Palmer with that cold sense of having been bypassed by some ghostly spirit and unsure of what he had experienced.

"Sinclair? Hampton?" Palmer said loudly, waiting for the army and marine sergeants to report to him.

"The Sultan is to remain here," he said, indicating a strong point by the doors, "with two Foxes. Take the other two to the gate and switch off the engines. Hampton? Perimeter patrols in opposing directions, if you please."

The sergeants acknowledged their orders, gave their own to make it happen, and Palmer waited.

———

"There and there," said one engineer, his accent alien in the English countryside, "we need to access that panel and recalibrate, then reset the coolant flow from up there," he finished, pointing to a glass bubble on the walkway level above their heads.

The four men of the SAS patrol listened, but in honesty cared little for the technicalities as they wouldn't be asked to perform the task and thought it better to keep to their areas of expertise. They kept their weapons ready as the two Americans went about their work, draining the coolant and powering down the output to a more manageable level. The mostly-depleted coolant had drained away and the large pipes whooshed as more water pumped in. The two men worked for almost forty minutes, far less time than Downes expected, before declaring that they were done.

"That's it?" he asked them.

"Sure, all we had to do was drain the system, power it down as much as possible and top off the tanks," he replied, "This place is only kicking out about thirty percent of normal, but it's good for almost a year before we have to do anything to it. It ain't like there are a lot of folks around here using their microwaves, right?" he finished with a laugh.

"Nah, mate," Smiffy said acidly, "because most people in our fuckin' country are dead, so show a bit of respect."

The man shut his mouth, packed up his tools, and waited to be led back outside.

"Captain?" Downes said as he looked up to where Palmer was sprouting out of the hatch on the Sultan.

"Sir?"

"Is your man linked to your base?" Downes asked, wanting to know if they had open radio communication.

"He is," Palmer told him.

"Could you trouble them for our transport to be sent?" Downes enquired politely.

Palmer frowned, "Of course, but," he said hesitantly, "aren't you hitching a ride back with us?"

"They are," Downes said as he gestured to the engineers, "we're not."

He said nothing else, telling Palmer that the subject was, at least as far as the irregular soldiers of the special forces were concerned, closed. Palmer instructed his radio man to make the call and received his own orders to return to the island. Palmer offered to remain until such time as the helicopter arrived for the four-man team, but Downes quietly embarrassed him by pointing out that anything following the noise trail would be after them and not the aircraft it would never find. He didn't embarrass himself further by enquiring where they were going but wished the men well as he recalled his convoy to prepare to depart.

"Don't worry, Captain," Downes said with a chilling smile that was probably meant to seem reassuring, "something tells me we'll be meeting again soon."

———

Long before the convoy returned, Johnson found himself

summoned by the new commander of their island to deal with a civilian matter. He entered the room to find Colonel Tim looking remarkably flustered and the three men of his entourage seemingly powerless to assist.

"Thank God for that," said a young woman who appeared to be the spokesperson for the three civilians sitting at the table, "someone with some sense at last. Mister Johnson, would you please explain to this man that we aren't soldiers and that the army doesn't own us?"

Johnson turned to his new commanding officer and saluted, which seemed to please the man.

"Miss Perkins, perhaps if I understood the issue better?" he said gently, meaning that he had no damned clue what was happening.

"This gentleman," Kimberley said as she gestured towards the rather deflated-looking Colonel, "wants us all herded up and catalogued. Perhaps we should have serial numbers tattooed on our arms to make life easier for you?"

"Sergeant Major," Colonel Tim interrupted in what he thought was a placatory tone but in fact bathed the room in arrogance and condescension, "all I simply said was that we need to record the details of every civilian living under our protection here so that we can properly establish who can be of service."

"That's not what he said," Kimberley explained in a mirroring tone of talking down to him before glancing back at Johnson, "he said that we are all, what was it? Suckling at the military teat? And that we have to show our gratitude."

Johnson understood. He understood the point that both people were trying to make and was firmly of the opinion that the elderly buffoon understood no concept of speaking to an audience that wasn't disciplined and dutybound to call him Sir and follow his orders.

"Perhaps, Miss Perkins," he enquired politely, "if the

Colonel and I could discuss military matters in private for a moment?"

Kimberley understood, gave a nod to the two men there in support of her, who looked similarly offended, and retrieved a cigarette and lighter from her purse before stepping outside.

"May I, Sir?" Johnson asked, gesturing at a vacant chair.

"By all means, Johnson, by all means," the Colonel responded.

Johnson sat, cast a cold glance at the two orderlies, which clearly translated as a polite request for them to make themselves scarce, and smiled at the officer. His aide, a Lieutenant who probably had an advanced qualification in senior officer babysitting, and a tenuous family connection to the royals which elevated him above his years and rank, remained standing behind his Colonel.

"Sir, I don't want to overstep, but if I may offer a solution to dealing with the civilians that would save time and allow you to concentrate on command matters instead?" Johnson said. The Lieutenant smiled, acknowledging a fellow smooth-talker.

"What do you have in mind?" Colonel Tim asked, leaning forward in anticipation.

"It's just that an officer from my squadron had done all the legwork before you arrived, Sir, and if you'll permit me to say, Sir, it's more of a junior officer's job, so that you can keep a tactical awareness of the situation as a whole, Sir, and be ready to lead us instead of being bogged down with the whys and wherefores of the rank and file, let alone the vagaries of civilian management," he said, baffling the man's brain with what seemed like the witchcraft of the working classes. He had used this trick more than once in his career when dealing with officers and spouting total rubbish with a confident tone and a hopeful smile at the end of his official-sounding waffle never failed to confuse any senior officer.

"Ah, I see," the Colonel said as he leaned back and gave a

theatrically conspiratorial wink, "so you think this man would be better placed to smooth the waves, eh? Manage the herd a little?"

"Absolutely, Sir," Johnson said with a smile, happy that the man had seen the logical suggestion in his utter nonsense.

"Very well, I trust you'll see to that?" he asked as he craned his neck up to his aide.

"Of course, Sir, I shall seek out this…" he trailed off as he shot a questioning look at Johnson.

"Lieutenant Simpkins-Palmer, Sir," he answered, investing the objectionable, jumped-up brat of an officer's name with as much aristocratic idiocy as he could muster.

"I shall find him right away, assuming he can be spared from his duties," the aide replied.

Johnson was dismissed and watched as the Colonel stepped outside and slipped on his cap to clasp his hands behind his back and enjoy a relaxing stroll back down the hill, seemingly without a care in the world. Johnson followed, stopped next to Kimberley Perkins and glared at the two orderlies, who were also smoking and standing close to the civilian woman.

"Well?" he asked them, "Off you fuck, lads."

They scurried away after their Colonel, eager to flee the big warrant officer, even if they didn't fall directly under his command.

He turned to face the three civilians as soon as they were alone.

"I'm sorry about that," he said formally.

"That's quite alright, Sergeant," said a man who Johnson guessed was perhaps in his early fifties. He bridled at the unintentional demotion the man gave him and tried to ignore it.

"You'll have Lieutenant Palmer back acting as a buffer between yourselves and the new Colonel," he said, feeling as though he was betraying his beloved British Army ever so slightly, "but I rather suspect that the man wants to feel more useful…"

"We understand, Mister Johnson," Kimberley said to mollify the conversation, "and I apologise that you were called into that, but I suspected it might have got out of control had we not sent for you," she said as she self-consciously brushed her hair down over the left side of her face, as she did often.

It was only then that the Squadron Sergeant Major, a man who prided himself on being astute and living in the world between the lines, realised that the Colonel had not sent for him to control the unruly civilian population, but rather that the civilians had sent for him to assist them. He wasn't entirely sure what that meant for the time being, so he squared it away until he could figure it out. He opened his mouth to say that he would provide Lieutenant Palmer with specific instructions, but his words were stopped in his throat.

"Sergeant Major," Kimberley said as she watched him out of the right side of her face, turning the left side away self-consciously, "we are having an informal meeting tonight to discuss matters. I wonder if you would join us? The Royal Arms at five?"

Johnson was taken aback by the sudden invitation but managed to keep his face from showing it. He regained his composure and said that he would try to make it if duty allowed.

Embarrassed, he made his way to find the younger Palmer and tell him exactly what he needed to do.

EIGHTEEN

Peter and Amber woke again that morning and went through the same routine of eating breakfast and feeding the cat, who had returned undetected at some point. The house itself was comfortable and secure, and there was enough food for another two days at least, but the water situation meant that they would be forced to find somewhere new that day.

He told Amber this, and thought it was remarkable how such a young kid could take bad things happening in her stride without complaining. She didn't cry, she didn't complain or refuse to help, she just nodded and got on with everything.

Peter filled his water bottle before they left, using a small cup to decant the water from the toilet cistern to pour it in a bit at a time, and then he asked Amber if she needed to use the toilet one last time before they left.

She screwed up her face in thought, rolled her eyes up toward her left brow, and pursed her lips before finally nodding that she did. Peter smiled at her, finding her silent ways of communicating with him both funny and endearing, and placed a hand on her head without thinking as she walked past. She didn't respond to the touch, and Peter didn't even register that he had done it, such was the strength of the protective bond he felt for the girl already.

It was as though she was more than just another person who had survived, it was as though he had saved her life, which he reckoned he had because there'd been one of the things coming for the door when he'd found her, and that somehow made her his responsibility.

She was his burden, but not with any sense of regret or reluctance. Her survival had somehow become his life's mission overnight, and the thought of abandoning her or failing in that mission was simply unthinkable to him. Amber was now his sole purpose in life, as he didn't seem to have any other pressing engagements on his calendar.

His musings had gone on so long that she had returned downstairs from the bathroom and stood level with his stomach and smiled up at him briefly.

She was ready to go.

Peter had fed the cat, unloading two cans of food onto plates for it to give it a head start after they left. The window was left partly open, and they shut the back door after themselves when they left. The cat hadn't come back after breakfast to say goodbye to them.

Peter had loaded up his backpack with as much of the heavier stuff as possible, leaving Amber with the shopping bag to manage. That kept his hands free to wield the pitchfork and he crouched low to stalk along the rear path and around the side of the house. They saw nothing moving in the village, but Peter thought their luck had been pushed sufficiently to warrant moving on. Plus, he couldn't guarantee that there was any more water in the other houses. He looked up into the overgrown hedge, lifting the weapon to move a sprig of a leafy branch out of the way of the road sign.

Fingerboard, his mind told him out of nowhere when he saw it. He guessed that name, wherever he had heard it, made sense as it was like a finger telling him how far it was to the next place and in what direction.

The fingerboards gave him a choice of two places, both of which his inbuilt sense of direction said were okay, as he hadn't been to them yet. One said four and a half miles, written in numbers and fractions, the other said two and three quarters. Looking down at Amber's little legs, he chose the second place and pointed out their direction to her. She said nothing, not that he expected her to, and just started stepping off in that direction. He set off beside her, both of them walking in the middle of the road, Peter sweeping his eyes left and right as they went. He looked down at her out of the corner of his eye, marvelling that someone so little could walk so well, given what she had been through.

A high-pitched whine pierced the upper limits of his hearing, making his body tense in anticipation and his breathing grow rapid, ready to move if he had to. Before he had a chance to make a decision, a screaming, blurry dark monster erupted overhead and shot over them at a deceptively low altitude. He expected it to blow them violently with a downwash, but instead only the noise reached them. Both of them flinched and ducked lower, as though the flying monster was much, much lower than it was.

As quickly as it had burst into their world it was gone again, straight over their heads and out of sight in another heartbeat, leaving behind it a brief, violent memory and the fading scream of the engines. The two children straightened and looked at one other, Peter with an open mouth and wide eyes and Amber with a shrug and a look of bewildered amusement.

Unable to think of anything appropriate to say for the occasion, Peter looked around their surroundings instead, in case anything unwelcome also wanted to see where the big, fast-moving helicopter had disappeared to.

They had walked for what his blue and red watch face told him was just over thirty minutes, when they stopped and now Peter saw a footpath intersecting the route they were on. The path to their left dropped down a slight hill to where the very tops of chimneys showed. He glanced back to the road, reading from the direction of the trees ahead that the road looped to the left. At least he guessed it did. He looked at the distant building down the sloping path, back to the road and back again as he tried to figure out whether to risk the shortcut. As he was close to figuring it out, a small hand tugged at his trouser leg.

He looked down to Amber, a sinking feeling in his chest, and wondered what fresh hell was heading their way. She pointed back down the road in the direction they had come from, and he squinted to see what she had.

"What is it?" he asked her.

In response she just shook her outstretched finger in the same direction, meaning that he should look instead of talking. He squinted his eyes, straining to see anything until a flash of dark movement made his breath catch in his throat.

Until he realised what it was.

"Ha!" he blurted out loudly in shocked amusement. Amber let out a small giggle as he realised what her sharp eyes had already seen.

Tail raised vertically and curled over at the very tip, the black and brown cat popped out of the long grass of the verge and trotted towards them.

It meowed when it got close, walked straight in between their legs and began snaking around Amber as it rose up off its front paws to purr loudly and rub its cheek against her hand. Amber looked up at Peter, her eyes asking the question that her lips would not. Peter shrugged, seeing no possible way he could even enforce leaving the cat behind if he wanted to, and not having the heart to say no anyway.

I guess I'm just collecting strays now, he thought to himself with mock annoyance.

"Come on, then," he said to both of them, and climbed the wooden posts in the hedgerow break to follow the footpath down the slope. He turned and reached out for Amber to pass him her bag, sticking the pitchfork into the dirt so that it stood up vertically, then held out his other hand after she had passed over the bag to help her over. She took his hand unthinkingly, much the same way as a child would when crossing the road with a grown up, but the small gesture of trust and the warmth of her hand made him feel better somehow.

After they had climbed over, they turned to look at the cat, who just stared at them blankly from the other side. Peter spoke to it, offering encouragement like it was a younger sibling who was refusing to walk another step. Amber make a kissing noise with her lips and patted her legs. The cat stared at both of them before abruptly craning its neck over its left shoulder to lick itself.

"Come on," Peter told the girl, "if it's followed us this far, it'll follow us the rest of the way."

Amber seemed to consider this and shrugged again, picking up her bag again ready to move. When they reached the outskirts of the village after another twenty minutes of walking down the gently sloping field, they found that the path they were on emerged into a graveyard. Peter's back crawled, threatening to make him shudder. His only experience of zombies was of them as cartoon characters, and then they were usually comedy characters with a hilariously low intelligence and easily foiled by the animated hero of the programme he was watching. They were always represented as bursting out of their graves one hand at a time and shuffling off in search of brains, which made him question the effectiveness of burial in the first place.

Weren't people in coffins when they were buried? How did

they get out and stand up under the weight of the soil? How shallow were the graves in these cartoons and why did they have green skin and crazy eyes?

Thought of the eyes sobered him. Maybe some of the cartoons had been right, only they hadn't known or hadn't told the truth that instead of being funny characters, they were relentless and terrifying if they gathered in more than pairs. Flashbacks came to him of the mob, the horde of things who blew through his home and devoured everything living except him, through his quick actions and dumb luck.

Maybe the cartoons should have shown the zombies as people the characters knew, maybe their best friend, and made them watch as they burned up and died and then got up and ripped the heroes apart with their hands and teeth.

Shaking those dark thoughts away, he looked for a way to skirt the graveyard and found a small stone bridge over a tiny trickle of a brook which he could easily have jumped. Amber couldn't, he guessed, so he led her over the little bridge.

"Trip, trap, trip, trap…" she whispered from the bank behind him as he walked over the narrow stones. Peter froze, instantly recalling the tale of the three billy goats and the troll under the bridge. His feet woke up before his brain and he stepped fast over the bridge and turned to snatch Amber up but saw that she had stopped before the bridge and was pointing down.

A hand, pale and bloated with wet skin peeled away from where the blackened fingernails clawed at the bridge to haul a naked and milky-eyed monstrosity from the shallow water below.

The first thought to strike him and run through his brain almost conversationally, was about the exact circumstances that had led to a person who had turned into one of them being, at least mostly from what he could see, naked and hiding under a tiny stone bridge by a graveyard in a village with maybe twenty buildings. He wondered what possible scenario could have led to this happening, and he found himself at a total loss for a logical explanation.

As this flash of thought ran through his brain, roughly a second had passed in the real world, and in that second, the pale and bloated skin of the thing's head rose up out of the shallow water with globules of green algae plastered to its face and partly obscuring its mouth. Then, and possibly worst of all, the thing that struck him next was the smell.

Afterwards, much afterwards in fact, he decided to re-categorise what he had experienced at that moment and classified the smell as something worse than a stench, but not quite a foul taste. It was definitely up there with the time on the farm he had to try and stay quiet with half of his mouth containing mud and slime which was mostly animal shit, and he reckoned it might have actually been worse.

Instead of wasting time considering all of these illogical and irrelevant thoughts, he decided to thrust out the pitchfork and solve the problem before it became any worse than a fright and a disgusting smell. As he lined up the weapon, the bloated mess let out a hiss that was mostly a gargle through a clogged mouth, but it was answered with another hiss of pure venom and aggression.

On the low wall next to Amber, the cat had caught up and was voicing its opinion about the situation. Peter knew that cats had a much better sense of smell than humans, so he couldn't even begin to imagine what the cat felt about the bloated floater.

Before the situation devolved any further, the pitchfork's prongs entered the thing's head just before and just behind its left ear and ended the grand entrance before it had chance to get into full flow.

Peter withdrew the weapon with a grunt and a sharp pull, and the repulsive lump flopped back into the low, murky water.

The cat had stopped hissing but stayed utterly motionless and kept its eyes on the thing, with only twitches of a hugely puffed-up tail betraying that it wasn't a statue. Amber just looked blankly at him.

Then he remembered the warning she'd given him, as cryptic as it was, and he held out a hand for her to cross over to him. She didn't hesitate and skipped across the bridge lightly to join him, then looked back at the cat who hopped down and stalked over the bridge to follow.

"How did you know?" he whispered to her as his head swivelled to locate any other unwelcome surprises, "Did you see it?" he asked, worrying that he had looked and hadn't seen it there. She didn't answer, so he stole a glance at her to check. She shrugged, a genuine '*I don't know*' shrug and smiled back at him.

Peter didn't know what he expected, so he guessed the shrug was what he deserved. He pointed at her, then to his side and waited for her to nod. Stalking out into the road with her beside him, he crept along in the open so as not to be surprised by any more jack-in-the-box zombies in close quarters. He made for the largest house he could see, stopping once to listen intently as Amber stood still in total silence as though she wasn't even breathing. The cat had disappeared again but that was hardly his priority at that point.

He saw three cars parked on the road at nearby houses which seemed to be so old in construction that they didn't have driveways and noticed something was somehow *off* about them. They were at unnatural angles, because people usually parked their cars vaguely straight. Their wing mirrors were bent backwards or pushed in, depending on whether he could see the front or the back of the cars, and all of them were smeared with dried streaks of black.

Sneaking towards the house and the taller than average front door, he pointed for Amber to wait on the other side of the big car and waited until she moved. Exchanging a look, he left her there and tried the front door.

He'd once seen a television programme where the woman with big curly hair claimed that crime was up so high that people were afraid to leave their doors unlocked any more. That struck Peter as a stupid thing to say, because if locks weren't necessary, why did every door have them? Personally, he was glad to live in the country for two reasons. One, the only city he had ever been to was London, which had burned down in riots a month ago, from what he had seen on the news, and two, around there a lot of people actually *did* leave their doors unlocked.

The big house was one of them. He turned the round, brass doorknob and was rewarded by protesting springs until a click denoted it was open. Pushing it gently inwards, he stood back two paces and raised the pitchfork.

"Hello?" he called into the house as loud as he dared, and hearing no reply. He looked over to Amber, seeing the top of her head from the nose up as she peered over the front of the car, and tried to figure out what to do, to try and decide whether he should take her inside on a house search and put both of them at risk if they had to run away.

Just then, he realised what the signs outside had meant, and what had happened there. It also went some way to explaining how a naked zombie found itself stuck in a low brook, and he knew in that instant that there wouldn't be a single one of them there unless it was trapped.

That horde which had nearly consumed him in a flood, that swarm of corpses that had steamed across the countryside like a roller had been through here in some form. It had filled that road outside and swept inexorably onwards, and anything that was free to shuffle or walk or crawl would have been taken along with it. With renewed confidence in his logic, he called out louder into the house.

"Oi," he yelled, "zombies!"

He smiled to himself as he said it, knowing that he was showing off for Amber and not caring. He smiled because it was the first time he had used the word out loud and when he did, it seemed to take some of the fear and stress out of the situation.

Nothing happened inside the house, so he waved her to him and walked inside. It had five bedrooms, an office, wardrobes that seemed more like bedrooms in size, without windows, and a door to another room where the washing machine and a tumble drier were built into the same worktops as the kitchen had. There was a door from that room that led into the big garage where there were tools and camping things and an old car with no roof.

He checked every room, every cupboard and every possible place that a person could hide in, as though it was a high-stakes hide and seek tournament.

Loser gets eaten, he thought grimly, but he was right, and the house was empty.

As impressive as it was, as huge and luxurious as the kitchen was, which he guessed was about the same size as the entire ground floor of his old house, it yielded about a day's worth of food for them, which meant that he would have to check the other houses in the village. He was happy to do that, hell he'd been doing it for a few weeks before he met Amber, but at least he would have somewhere for her to stay when he went. The one good thing was that the garage contained plastic bottles of water, which meant that they wouldn't be drinking from toilet cisterns for a while.

They roamed the house looking for things and Peter checked the flow of the taps to see if they worked, purely out of interest. To his utter disbelief, and by some miracle, the tap he turned flowed strongly with water.

Water that, to his great delight, was getting hot.

NINETEEN

"Ward, where are we with comms?" Hadlington asked, with a hint of desperation in his voice.

"Still nothing, Sir," she said coolly, but inside she was screaming for a way to warn the two teams of SAS and SBS that they were heading directly into a complete shit storm. She blamed the Americans, naturally, as they had been late in relaying the information to their own command, who had then passed it directly on to the land-based control room for that area. Had the information come only thirty minutes earlier, she could have contacted the helicopter pilot and ordered the abort, but the teams were on the ground and totally unaware what was coming for them.

"Fucking hell," Hadlington swore under his breath, "get me command," he told her, "and send a runner to fetch me the Colonel. I need him to sign an order for these men to drive into the lion's den."

———

The four men comprising Charlie-One-One had climbed in

silence back aboard the helicopter that had been sent for them and held on to the hanging straps as the bird's nose tipped towards the east and powered away. Technically they weren't *back* on board, as this helicopter, while being the same model, was a fully-fuelled one that had come via a gentler speed as their first ride was blasting back to its floating home. This one was tasked with dropping them off in south London, where they were due to rendezvous with Charlie-One-Two, who were infiltrating up the Thames, no doubt in order to provide additional options should any team have an issue getting in or out. The team and their boats would have been inserted by helicopter in the wider stretches of the river to the east for them to slip into the city quietly.

The other team had been at their own small base on the south coast when the shit hit the fan, and as they were so few in number, they were forced to take to the Channel in their rigid inflatable boats to escape the enemy masses on dry land. When the navy began to congregate in the relatively narrow waterway between the English and French coasts, they were picked up and rapidly portioned off into individual patrols to be made available for use wherever command saw fit.

Of that four-man team, two had seen warfare in the East Falklands in 1982 and constantly reminded the others of that. All of them were formerly Royal Marines, as were all troopers of their four squadrons, but one had taken the unusual route of joining first the Royal Navy, before becoming enamoured with the elite reputation of the marines. He had quit after four years because he was told there was no possible way to transfer. His branch had been at manning balance, and not surplus, so there was no way he could transfer, he was told. So he had left, signed out and walked off base to go straight into the forces careers office to sign on as a Royal Marine recruit, then waited in cheap accommodation outside Plymouth for five weeks until the next recruitment process began. It never occurred to him that he wouldn't pass recruitment and selection.

That confidence, which some of the training staff saw as arrogance, saw him through the Commando course and onto an accelerated path to his first promotion, due to his previous experience and capabilities. Some thought him career-driven, but those who worked with him knew him to be all work at work, and all play outside. After another four years in a new coloured beret, he again had his head turned when his unit had encountered members of the UK Special Forces in Northern Ireland.

They were kept separate in the barracks, with its anti-mortar mesh and high walls, and they were ordered not to talk to them or ask about their activities. He had disobeyed that order, finding a man who had greeted some of the older marines in his unit. Finding out that the man had previously been one of them, he asked him outright who he was with.

The Special Boat Service became his next goal, and his request for selection followed as soon as he returned to the UK. In his usual style he passed selection on his first attempt, relishing the gruelling physical and mental pressure of being tested beyond the expected limits of human performance and resolve.

Now, despite his previous experience and time spent as a special forces soldier, he was still referred to as The Matelot. Alex Bufford, Sergeant Special Boat Service, preferred to be called Buffs. He was tall, fit and strong as one would expect from a former marine, but he found that the majority of his fellow special forces soldiers were often short and wiry, in contrast to his big shoulders and thick arms. His strength was overt, whereas others seemed more like tough goats or ants that seemed able to lift ten times their own body weight.

Buffs, a newly-minted Sergeant through exceptionally hard work, led his team of four in two rigid inflatable boats up the filthy Thames river, which was thick with floating corpses that bobbed on the surface, bloated and rotting. Their engines were only turning at less than half their capacity for two reasons: to keep a lower noise profile and to allow them to avoid the worst concentrations of dead bastards. On more than one occasion they were forced to power up and then lift their propellers from the water to bump over the bodies without blending them.

With two men in each boat they were well below capacity, but the likelihood was that they were their own 'exfil' and a rescue was about as possible as finding a decent bar open in the city.

They found the small pier they wanted by the GPS co-ordinates and cut their engines in unison to float the rest of the way in silence. Tying off their crafts, they slipped onto dry land and stalked effectively forwards as their guns came up to cover all angles.

Straight ahead, third right, second left, first right, first right, he repeated to himself, going over the map in his head which correlated to the one in his leg pocket. The map was totally unmarked and folded to its original lines so as not to even betray the area they were operating in, in case they were captured. Operational habits of basic mission secrecy were so deeply ingrained in them that even the inability of their enemy to read a map would not encourage procedure to be abandoned.

They made the turns on his lead, taking each turn as they had in training and real-life, until they reached the innocuous double doors of their target location.

A bird noise, piercing and subtle yet alien to the environment, sounded to their right. It came from a fire-damaged corner of a building on the first floor, where the partly destroyed glass offered a wide view of the street below. Buffs stopped and dropped to one knee, looking up at the window not at anything he could see, but at the place where he would have placed his own team if he had arrived first.

"One-Two," he said softly, waiting for a response.

"One-One, coming down," came the reply, before the slightest shirt in the shadows moved behind the damaged glass. Moments later four men emerged dressed and equipped similarly to them, with the addition of beards that only served to make their eyes seem brighter, as they were framed by unruly darkness.

The man at their point nodded to him in a curt but efficient greeting, then stopped to take a knee beside him.

"Downes, Hereford," he introduced himself.

"Bufford, Poole," Buffs responded.

Pleasantries exchanged, they stepped through the double doors and slowly descended the steps towards the underground lab that nobody knew was there, let alone responsible for the end of days. They clicked on the bright torches attached to their weapons to illuminate the pitch black where sunlight could not penetrate and found the outer door of the lab.

The MP5 had no bayonet, so dispatching the single lurching corpse who stood resting its face against the thick security glass of that door could not be done at distance unless with a bullet. Given that even suppressed shots make noises, especially in cavernous underground areas, Buffs dropped his weapon to hang on its strap and held up a hand to signal the other seven men not to fire. Just as the zombie turned in response to the approaching lights and footfalls to leave part of its face glued to the glass and expose bright white bone on its forehead, Buffs slipped the small pioneer axe from the belt loop on his right hip and swung the small weapon to bury the pointed end downwards into the skull of the creature to crumple it down to the ground.

Downes watched with evident respect for the display and the weapon, using his weapon-mounted torch to regard the short-handled axe to see a brightly polished head smeared with dark gore. The axe had clearly been a display piece somewhere, but questions about it would have to wait. He stepped forwards and tapped repeatedly on the glass until a suspicious pair of wild eyes set in a dishevelled face appeared.

"Open. The fucking. Door," Downes said slowly, with a visible finger pointed downwards to the lock, carefully mouthing each word until the unmoving man inside finally snapped into reality and turned a ship-style handle inside to unseal it.

The eight men stepped inside, weapons up and scanning as they fanned out to search the collection of rooms, which stank beyond compare. It was not enough to assume that the lab was made safe just because someone else was in there, they had to see for themselves.

"Professor Grewal?" Downes asked, placing a hand on the shoulder of the man and crouching slightly to try and force eye contact, "Professor Sunil Grewal?" he tried again, with a shake as Buffs closed the door behind them.

"Sunny," Grewal said, as he seemed to emerge back into consciousness. Downes winced at the man's breath.

"Okay, Sunny, we're getting you out of here. Do you have the samples?" he asked.

Grewal nodded and pointed to a large specialist case. Downes nodded to one of his troopers, who picked the case up with evident difficulty.

"Mac?" he said, then, hearing the response from behind him, "find the computers."

Mac did, tipping over the heavy desktop units and smashing open their cases and prising out the huge internal drives. Dezzy was collecting all of the $3\frac{1}{2}$ inch floppy discs and stuffing them into a black bag indiscriminately, while Smiffy began to pour acrid smelling fuel onto key things such as paperwork. Meanwhile, two of Buffs' team assisted by piling things into easier piles.

Just then, the telephone on the wall rang a shrill chirping noise. Grewal giggled to himself, as though the telephone being real was a sudden shock to him, and Buffs picked it up.

A short conversation ensued, during which pertinent questions were asked.

"How big? …Location? …Direction? …How long? …Understood."

Just as he replaced the handset and opened his mouth, a shout came from the door they had come through.

"Company," was all it said, and company didn't come close to accurately describing what was out there.

"How many?" Buffs asked in a low voice, considering whether the two teams could cover the mile through the city to their boats and get out ahead of the leading edge of the wave. Eight men and one civilian who would probably need carrying, he imagined, along with the heavy sample case.

Left, left, second right, third left, straight ahead to the boats, he thought to himself as he mapped the return journey in his mind. Just as the answer told him that making a run for it was out of the question.

"Err, all of the fuckers, I think," came the bleak response.

Because the swarm was already in the city.

TWENTY

The AWACS patrolling the area had been diverted towards Poland, where the Soviets were apparently performing heavy carpet bombing of the whole eastern edge of the country to create a no-man's-land of death and rubble in a desperate bid to prevent the disease from walking into the motherland. The bombing, the incessant mortar and artillery fire, had served only to attract every hungry dead person on the European continent towards them, and it was becoming a question of what would run out first; the enemy or the ordnance.

While that report was fed back to the US via their carrier fleet just outside the English Channel, the early-warning aeroplane had its eyes off the mainland UK.

The mission to recover the virus research from London had come via joint command but was a direct order from the US forces, and moreover, came from people who did not give their name with an order; simply where they worked. In this instance, 'Century House' gave the orders, meaning British foreign intelligence was calling the shots, despite its UK headquarters seemingly overrun and abandoned.

It was simply beyond the paygrade of any one of the military personnel involved to know the truth that the outbreak was as a direct result of poor containment protocols, after the US and UK governments collaborated to produce a biological weapon to use as a doomsday option and an alternative to nuclear bombardment in the Cold War against the socialist states in the east.

Had that AWACS been watching the south east of England, they would undoubtedly have seen the gathering swarm moving fast back toward the city for no explicable reason, along with another massing in Bristol. The swarming seemed to be cyclical and unpredictable, but there weren't enough eyes and too many things to watch.

The information came again too late from the American satellite images, but the real-time information told a far more worrying story.

Out in the Channel the response to the swarms started too late, and the desperate rush to recall the teams on the ground failed to make contact. The next plan was to send in a rescue, and that was where the control team on the ground was employed.

———

"Palmer!" Major Hadlington shouted as he jogged awkwardly towards the returning convoy, waving a piece of paper that the captain suspected was a signed order, "Palmer!"

"What on earth does this buffoon want?" Palmer asked himself out loud as the hatless intelligence officer stomped to a halt beside his wagon.

"Palmer, you need to turn around!" he yelled, somewhat inappropriately in Captain Palmer's opinion.

Palmer climbed down and stood beside the major, wearing a look of annoyed confusion.

"Captain," Hadlington said intensely, "we need to deploy to London immediately, in force."

Palmer, ignoring the *we* part and deciding that he had the right to know why, turned to the officer, "Major, I'm sure there is a perfectly good reason, which I must ask…"

"Because there is an eight-man special forces team stuck in an underground laboratory with a scientist who may be able to shed light on the virus that's *fucking up our country*," he hissed angrily through gritted before getting himself under control, "because there is another swarm coming for them, because we have been ordered to, because we *have* to. Don't you understand, man? This could be a *cure!*"

Palmer stared at him for a beat, then turned and fired off a string of orders.

"Sergeant Sinclair," he bawled with confidence and alacrity, "your troop to remain here as guard with Three Troop. Send runners for Mister Johnson and the troop sergeants immediately. Sergeant Swift?"

"Captain?" came the reply from the building used as the gatehouse.

"Can I trouble you to get on the radio and have the re-supp fuel wagon here right away?" he said, giving the order politely and making Swift feel as though he was doing the young officer a personal favour.

"Sinclair? Unload all your spare *seven-six-two* ready for the outgoing troops. Sir?" he said as he wheeled back to the surprised, moustached man in spectacles, "Where precisely are we going?"

———

Maxwell was recruited by Johnson for support and the two of them entered the Royal with more trepidation than they had going out into the apocalypse. They gave their name and rank to the landlord, who was keeping a full tab of the army's expenses for later reimbursement in the hopeful wish that the world would get back to normal one day.

The men gave their thanks for their pint of mild bitter and joined two women who were waving politely to them.

Johnson gave Maxwell a sideways look, suspecting an ambush, as one of the women was Maxwell's wife. They took the two spare stools at the round wooden table, the offered greetings were exchanged, and Kimberley Perkins brushed her hair down across her face as she always did when speaking to people.

"I'm so sorry, I forgot to ask, how is your chap who got hurt?" she said to the two soldiers.

"He's on the mend, thank you," Maxwell said, "but it's not us responsible, is it, my love?" he said to his wife with a genuine warm smile.

"Oh? You didn't tell me you were on the payroll, Denise?"

Maxwell's wife shrugged and smiled self-effacingly, "We all have to do our bit," she said, then shook her packet of ciga-rettes and slid two out to offer one to Kimberley without checking to see if she even wanted one. That subtle gesture told Johnson that the two women knew each other far better than they were letting on. Maxwell, saying nothing about not being offered one of his wife's cigarettes, simply helped himself to the packet and frowned to find it empty. The two women shared a single flame from a lighter and Denise Maxwell's eyes showed amusement at her husband.

Maxwell tutted with an exaggerated eye roll and produced a packet of rolling tobacco and papers.

"Have a tailor-made," Kimberley said with a smile and slipped a packet out of her handbag, which hung on the side of the chair she occupied. Maxwell thanked her, put one in his mouth and thumbed another up for Johnson. He declined, not feeling the urge for a smoke as he would surely be getting enough of the smell and taste from the three others.

"So, Mister Johnson," Kimberley said as she looked at him sideways, "what is happening in the wider world?"

"It's Dean," he said awkwardly as he invited her to use his first name to signify both that he considered himself off-duty and that he held no domain over the young civilian woman.

Maxwell smiled but was careful to keep that from his boss, who he had never called by his first name. Only a handful of times had Johnson had called him by his first name, and the two were simply satisfied with the army's habit of surnames. They were as close as any of the senior men in the squadron could be and were friends within the confines of their working restrictions.

"Well, Miss Perkins," Johnson began, "the Am…"

"Kimberley, please," she said, mirroring his own acceptance of informality with a smile that he was forced to mirror.

"Kimberley," he began again, almost bashful, "the Americans are in the Channel, the cloak and dagger brigade are up to their usual tricks, and we aren't going die from a nuclear power station breaking down. Other than that, I'm a mushroom," he finished with a deprecative shrug as he took a gulp of his beer.

Denise chuckled and leant towards Kimberley, "Mushroom," she explained, "means that he…"

"That he's being kept in the dark," Kimberley finished, intentionally leaving out the part about the bullshit.

They giggled at the men's reactions to the non-military woman's knowledge which the others attributed to the time she had spent around the men and families.

"Dean, I understand you aren't married?" Kimberley asked innocently.

Johnson almost spat his beer at the suddenness and the personal nature of the question. He wanted to counter with the questions about what had happened to her face, about the scars she tried to cover and where the hint of steel and tenacity in her character came from, but he didn't. Instead he coughed and shook his head in weak answer.

The conversation bounced around with a little less awkwardness after the ice breaker, until Denise gave their excuses and the two women went to the toilets together. On the way, they took up a conversation they'd been having before the men had joined them. Mostly it was speculation about where the Royal Family might be, and what had happened to them. More specifically, they were intrigued by Sarah Ferguson and Prince Andrew, their new baby girl and the state of their marriage.

Back in the bar, Johnson took another long pull on his beer, taking it past the halfway point and threatening to taste too good to stop after just one, then turned to Maxwell, who was similarly enjoying his pint.

"Is this your idea, or Denise's," he asked quietly with a hint of warning in his voice.

"Kimberley's," he responded with a smirk as he stubbed out his cigarette in the ashtray and raised his open hands in mock surrender, "we're just conscripts."

"You're taking the piss, right?" Johnson asked incredulously.

"Hand on heart, Guv."

Johnson stared at him. The girl had to be almost twenty years younger than him and he couldn't comprehend why she would have any interest in the old bull that he saw himself as. Just as the two women re-emerged, he was saved from being driven off the field of battle by the main door of the pub bursting inwards.

All eyes turned to the young trooper, red-faced and out of breath as he stood there panting. Johnson didn't press the man, didn't add fear of himself to the panic the trooper obviously already felt.

"Report to troops," he called into the pub, "senior NCOs to the bridge."

With that, he ran from the door, clearly needing to make his other calls at billets to rouse the men.

Johnson and Maxwell exchanged a look, mixed adrenaline and dread, and on Johnson's part, a hint of relief; going to work was safer than the situation he had been dropped into. They finished their pints with synchronised actions and offered brief apologies before they headed back down the hill at a steady jog via Johnson's billet where they had left their weapons and webbing. Arriving at the threshold of the bridge, they were met by running engines, running men, and an efficient looking Captain Palmer at the centre of everything.

"Ah, Johnson," he said as he saw the SSM approaching, not using the honorary 'Mister' in recognition of his warranted officer status and betraying that time was so short that even the impeccably-mannered Captain Palmer didn't have time to observe the proprietaries.

"And Maxwell," he added to the sergeant, "how many of your wagons are fit to go?"

"Three, Sir," he answered quickly, leaving out the irrelevant facts as to why one of the squadron's four Spartans was out of commission due to its gearbox being in the process of being rebuilt. Palmer nodded, turning back to Johnson.

"You and I in the Sultans, three crews from assault troop in the lead, and Strauss' men. Maxwell, I need two drivers to bring Saxons for an exfil mission."

"Sir?" Johnson said, "if I may?"

"Of course," Palmer said.

"I'll ride in your wagon, no point in taking another. What's our target?"

"South London," Palmer said, "one hundred and fifty miles. I'm having maps sorted but we're looking at at least six hours without obstructions, assuming the M3 motorway is passable. We'll need to roll in the dark for most of it, so we are looking at a dawn extraction. I'd love to take a Chieftain but I'm afraid time is of the essence and we need the armour there as soon as possible. Can I ask you to arrange for rations for the men?"

Johnson nodded, adding the number of men rapidly in his head and arriving at twenty-seven, then turned away to find a runner to send to the quartermaster and request fifty-four ration packs to be brought immediately. He told the runner to give his compliments to Lieutenant Lloyd and request some marines to assist him. Johnson's own mind spun up, calculating distances and allowing for an additional margin of error. Deciding that the fuel held in the vehicles cut the three-hundred-mile journey too fine.

Looking around for an NCO not preparing to leave in the convoy, his eyes landed on the RMP sergeant. He walked over to stand close to him, ensuring that there were none of the enlisted men around before asking him for a favour. He could have ordered him, but making a sergeant from another branch fetch and carry for him was bad form in his book.

"Tim," he said, "can some of your chaps do me a big favour and sort some full jerrycans for the wagons?"

Swift understood the request for both what it was, and how it was posed and fetched up four of his men to begin arranging the spare fuel.

Twenty minutes later, fully loaded and equipped, their convoy rolled out to head east with an exhausted Captain resting his eyes as Johnson took the helm for their rescue mission.

TWENTY-ONE

Peter woke early, not having seen or heard any sign of any dead people wandering around in the village. His bladder woke him, and he didn't want to wake the sleeping girl opposite him, so he slipped out of the upstairs playroom to creep downstairs to the toilet there. The cat, having followed them in the front door to check out their new accommodation, stood from its spot on Amber's bedding and arched its back in an exaggerated stretch, looked at him as he tiptoed to the door and evidently decided that it was too early to harass him for breakfast, so it curled up back against the girl to go back to sleep.

They had decided on the playroom and had manhandled two single mattresses into the room along with bedding. Peter had never felt overly comfortable sleeping inside a stranger's bed, and since their first awkward night together, the two had kept to the arrangement of sleeping in the same room. It felt like camping to him, and he had no idea what it felt like for her because she hadn't spoken since her eerie warning about the bridge.

He attributed the early wake-up to the plentiful supply of bottled water which he had hit hard to make up for the day's walking in the warmth. The house, despite its lack of food supplies, had been exactly what they needed and if his suspicions were right, the village itself should be all but clear of any zombies. He reckoned he would start clearing that day, bringing back the food and stuff they wanted or liked back to the house, and hopefully they'd be able to hold up there for longer than he normally could, given that the smell of living people seemed to attract them inexplicably to the houses he occupied.

As he stood and breathed out to release the stream into the toilet, he thought about the problems that would cause; perhaps they had to start refilling the empty bottles with their waste and wrapping up the solids to keep it from smelling and attracting unwanted attention.

Grabbing another bottle of water and a packet of custard cream biscuits, he went back upstairs to find Amber awake and stroking the cat. Her eyes flickered to him as he walked back in and then returned to the cat who stretched out lazily against her side and purred loudly without opening its eyes. Peter opened the biscuits and took a handful before putting the packet next to her.

"Need to start looking in the other houses today," he told her through a mouthful of biscuit. She nodded, chewing and still stroking the cat.

"And we need to find some cat food for you," he said, looking at the cat. In response it opened its eyes to regard him briefly with a look somewhere between loving contentment and judgemental loathing. He couldn't be sure.

They ate the biscuits for breakfast, then he emptied his backpack to allow him to carry the shotgun. He checked the road outside through the cracks in the curtains and saw nothing to raise any suspicion. Picking up the pitchfork from the side of the front door he turned to tell her to wait for him to come back. The words caught in his mouth as he saw her pulling the Velcro of her shoes tight and smiling at him expectantly.

She was ready too.

"No," Peter said, "you wait here, and I'll be back soon, okay?" he said reassuringly.

He turned to leave, but she cleared her throat and waved him towards her, then walked towards the utility area, glancing back to check he was following her. He wasn't, so she waved him forwards until he traipsed after her in confused interest. She walked through to the garage, moved a blue plastic sheet aside and wheeled forward a small trolley with a look of pride on her face.

Peter smiled at the look she gave him and thanked her, misunderstanding that she was trying to get him to take the cart to make it easier. He helped her lift it over the lip of the door and wheel it into the house, stopping her to go back inside the garage and pick up the blue and yellow can to spray the wheel bearings and keep the trolley silent. He thanked her again and let her wheel it towards the front door, then turned to take it from her, but instead she frowned and refused to hand it over. She scrunched up her face, giving him her best grumpy face, and stayed resolute until he relented.

"Fine!" he said. "But you do exactly what I say, okay?"

She beamed and nodded, turning the grumpy face into a satisfied one of triumph.

Emerging into the daylight, they moved slowly, pausing to listen at intervals before stepping out onto the road and walking towards the nearest house. The downstairs windows were closed, the curtains open and the scene inside appeared undisturbed, so Peter tried the front door.

Locked. He turned to Amber and pointed to the floor at her feet then turned the finger to point vertically downwards to indicate that she should stay where she was. Her eyes locked onto his illuminated in the morning sunshine, and for the first time in the few days he had known her, he saw that her eyes were a pale golden colour with a darker, almost coppery ring around the edges of her iris. Temporarily taken aback by her striking eye colour, he recovered and slipped around the back of the house to find a way in.

Amber waited, eyes and ears alert to any hazard, until the front door creaked open and Peter bowed to invite her inside. They checked the ground floor, all modern and open plan around a central fireplace and chimney, and Amber's eyes rested on a big armchair with a wooden handle on the side. She seemed to know what it was, to recognise it when Peter didn't, and he watched as she sat on the chair and tried to manipulate the lever but struggled to apply enough pressure to it. Peter helped, laughing gently as the chair tipped back and the lower part raised to support her little legs.

In response to the small noises they made, a thud and a moan answered from the ceiling above. Looking up, both children froze until Amber spoke again.

"Someone's been sitting in my chair," she whispered, drawing out the second to last word theatrically with raised eyebrows and glancing up to meet Peter's gaze.

———

They reached the western outer edges of the city around one in the morning. They had encountered knots of dead here and there but never in a group bigger than ten, so they didn't stop to dismount and deal with them or bother using the guns; they simply rolled through at a steady but maintainable pace, neither dawdled nor risked engine failure.

Captain Palmer, restored after an hour spent dozing in the cramped and uncomfortable interior of the command vehicle, called a halt and scanned the surroundings using night vision goggles out of the open hatch. He saw nothing but heard clear sounds in the far distance of what sounded to his ears like an artillery bombardment.

"Daniels," he said, ducking back into the interior, "call home and ask if the ordnance dropping on London is ours, will you?" Johnson's eyebrows did a dance as he tried to understand, then he poked his own head out of a hatch and turned his head as though his ears were the dish of a radar. Settling his eyes into the darkness past the city, he held his breath and stared into the night before abruptly dropping back down to agree.

"Bigger guns than we have," he opined, meaning the army. "Got to be from the water?"

"That was my assumption also, Sarn't Major," Palmer responded as he watched Daniels working the radio.

"Confirmed, Sir," Daniels said, exposing his ability to listen to two conversations at once, "Navy are bombarding Greenwich as a diversionary tactic to draw the crowd south to the Thames."

"Is it working?" Johnson asked him, seeing the man's eyes drift out of focus as he listened to his radio.

"Appears to be," he said, nodding.

"Appears to be?" Palmer repeated, catching Johnson's eye and exchanging a look that wasn't filled with confidence.

"Fuck it," Johnson said, "just roll in?"

"Fuck it indeed," Palmer said before calling into his own radio connected to the rest of his convoy, "Sergeant Maxwell, on your lead, proceed to target."

They proceeded on Maxwell's lead into the city before the sun began to break over the horizon dead ahead of them. Twice the control room on the island called them for updated progress reports, and twice they reported a slower time to target than expected, due to the congestion of the city.

Everywhere they looked out of the thin observation slits of thick glass they saw destruction. Buildings were burned out, shop fronts destroyed, and blacked skeletons of cars and bodies littered the streets, forcing them to take a constantly deviating path to keep moving. In the third wagon back, Johnson counted the turns to their target with each lurching movement backwards or forwards for him.

"Nearly there," he said, feeling the anticipation inside their vehicle heighten.

———

"Yes?" Downes snapped, picking up the phone from the wall to stop its shrill chirping. He listened for a few beats, then put the phone down without another word.

"Two minutes," he said, seeing the other seven soldiers rise and get ready for action. The ninth man in the underground lab stayed on the floor and whipped his head around in a desperate attempt to understand what was happening.

"What's going on?" he blurted out, struggling to his feet, "what's happening? We're not going out there, are we? What about them? We can't g…"

As the man began ranting, the noise growing in volume, Downes and Buffs exchanged a look. The look reminded the SBS man that the human part of the precious cargo was his responsibility. He stepped close to the wild Professor and locked him with a stare.

"Get a grip," he growled, "we have to go out there because we can't stay here. Someone is coming for us in less than two minutes, so be ready to move." He went to turn away and heard the intake of breath from the man, who was about to protest again. He whipped back and spoke savagely.

"Every time you make a noise you put the lives of everyone in here in danger, so shut the fuck up," he snarled. The Professor recoiled from him, shocked and scared.

"You can't talk to me like that, you're supposed to…"

"Do we look like palace fucking guards?" Buffs asked with overt hostility to control the man and force him into fearful compliance. "Our job is to get you and your research back, not look after your feelings, so get up, shut up and get ready to move."

He stood, keeping his eyes low and his mouth closed.

"Form up," Downes called, watching the men stack by the exit door as though they were doing counter-terrorism training. The last man called ready, the heavy box of samples and the terrified scientist nestled tightly between them, and they quite literally waited for the cavalry to arrive.

―――――

"Three hundred yards, left side, left side," came Maxwell's voice from the head of the convoy. The first light of dawn had burst over the tops of the high buildings and shone harsh rays into the concrete canyons of the city.

"First Saxon, stop after the red doorway, *red doorway,*" Palmer barked into the radio, "when stationary, all wagons fire at will."

Maxwell saw the doorway, overshot it intentionally to allow space for five vehicles behind to pass, then called the stop and spun the cupola to engage the shambling corpses approaching from the front. He cut them down with short, controlled bursts, not aiming to render them safe but just destroy their legs so that they couldn't get to them.

The two armoured personnel carriers came to a squealing halt with the back doors just past the entrance to the underground lab. All around, the sounds of heavy gunfire barked and echoed to confuse the ears of all but the most experienced warriors.

―――――

The eight men filed up the stairs two by two with their burdens being dragged with them. The last thing Mac did, at the tail of the group, was to spill the last of the inflammable liquid they had around the lab. At the top of the stairs he turned, made sure that the others were clear, pulled a grenade from his webbing and pulled the pin.

With an accurate but gentle underhand toss, he lobbed the small bomb to bounce off the second to last step and hit the door, intentionally left open at an angle, to skitter across the tiled floor and come to a rest.

The grenade exploded, spewing the white phosphorous filler to burn intensely and ignite the inflammable liquid and the piles of paper in a violent burst that blew hot air and scraps of debris out of the entrance and up to street level, hot on the heels of the running men. As Downes' men split left with their heavy box, and Bufford's turned right, the explosion erupted out of the stairwell behind them. The heavy double doors at the Saxons' rears were opened and men piled in, their MP5s making rapid popping noises as the covering men took rapid but measured shots at the closest zombies.

"Last man," came the twin shouts to tell the exposed soldiers that they could get inside the safety of the armoured cars. Almost simultaneously, the doors of both wagons closed and locked, and hands thumped the walls to tell the drivers to go.

The convoy revved their engines, gears were engaged, and the convoy started to roll forwards with their guns still spitting flame.

Palmer and Johnson exchanged a nod, neither of them outside the safety of their vehicle, as they alone could not bring their guns to bear without opening a hatch to use their pintle-mounted weapon. Daniels looked up expectantly, and Palmer told him to call it in.

They had their objective, and they were going home.

TWENTY-TWO

"Yes… I understand… and that's confirmed?" Commander Briggs said into the telephone that linked him on the bridge of the US Navy Destroyer to the Royal Navy aircraft carrier that he longed to be back aboard, "Yes… leave it with me," he finished, replacing the handset.

"Captain?" he said, politely getting the attention of the man in the big chair.

"Commander?" he drawled, one side of his moustache curling up to show his amusement. He could tell that the Brit hated being on his ship, hell anyone could tell that he hated it, but he enjoyed making the unsmiling man interact as much as possible.

"That was confirmation that the armour has the precious cargo," he said, not wanting to tell the captain that he didn't know precisely what that cargo was, but suspecting that the Americans knew more than he had been told about this mission, "However, they are likely to be intercepted by the second anomalous gathering heading southwest."

The captain knew what that meant, and Briggs was indeed correct in his assumption that information was compartmentalised and fragmented, with each person being given only the information that those above them thought they needed. He knew what the precious cargo was, as the man on board his ship who was appointed as a civilian government advisor had given him a top secret briefing on the contents of that London laboratory.

That man may as well have worn a baseball cap emblazoned with CIA, not that Langley's Mister Smith or Mister White, or whatever he wanted to call himself, would say as much.

"Commander," he said as he shifted in his chair and kept his eyes on the empty horizon, "I'm not up to speed with your British vagaries. Please define *likely to.*"

Briggs swallowed down his retort that the American military personnel he was forced to work with were all blunt instruments to a man, and instead he took a deep breath and tried to keep the weary hostility from his tone.

"Captain," he said carefully, "the swarm will almost certainly intercept the convoy before they regain the safety of their base, and even then, their safety can't be assured."

The captain stared at him for a moment before drawing in a theatrical breath through his nose as he shifted again onto the other buttock, making Briggs think that the man in charge of the vessel he had been pressed into service on was suffering with haemorrhoids. That thought made him smile, to know that the captain had a serious pain in the arse too.

"Helmsman, take us in close enough for shore bombardment. Crewman, get me command and advise them that it is my *strong* tactical recommendation that they launch a helicopter rescue. And get Castlemorton on the horn," he finished, preparing to deploy the most unlikely of weapons against the dead.

———

The radio in the administrative building of Castlemorton training area rang loud and long, leaving a persistent ringing tone in the ears of the Panzersoldaten of Two Platoon and Hauptmann Hans Wolff, their captain.

He stood, placing the perfectly moulded black beret on his head with its silver emblem of their mounts emblazoned on the badge, he stepped smartly to the telephone and picked it up.

"Ja, Hauptmann Wolff hier," he said, then frowned and listened, snapping his fingers and gesturing to the soldier nearest him for something to write on. The soldier scrabbled in the top pocket of his green-grey overalls and came up with a pad of paper and a stub of pencil. Wolff nodded and mm-hmm'd along to the voice on the other end of the line as he scratched numbers on the pad.

"Yes, I understand," he said in accented English, "of course, we will leave immediately. You too. Goodbye."

Hauptmann Wolff replaced the handset and breathed in deeply. He turned to his senior sergeant, Feldwebel Stefan Beck, and spoke solemnly.

"We have orders," he said formally in their native language, "we are now in this fight, and we leave immediately. Replace all ammunition with canister rounds, but keep a few high explosive and armour piercing just in case."

Beck stood and rearranged the crotch of his overalls, as uncomfortable in the clothing as they all were, and growled to clear his throat before the twenty men of their platoon. Four Leopard 2 tank crews and their four support soldiers were all that remained of their unit, who had been displaced from the training grounds in their own country by the tanks of the American and British squadrons. The huge spit of land in south Wales had reluctantly been their home, but at least it gave them the chance to hone their skills, driving and main-taining their beloved second generation Leopard tanks in that eager and perverse hope of every young soldier that they would get to see active service, and prove to everyone, but mostly to themselves, that they were a fine instrument of modern warfare.

"Wolfsrudel," Beck shouted, seeing all of their men smiling and bracing as he used the German for the Wolfpack, "weggetreten!"

Wolff watched as the men did as they were told and fell out to their duties, wearing grins as wide as the tracks of their tanks, and turned to his senior NCO.

"Beck," he said, with a slightly admonishing tone, "do try to remember not to call them that in front of our British allies, won't you?"

Beck, not dissuaded in the slightest, assured his officer that he would not call their men *Wolfpack* again. It was a term of endearment, of pride in their commander and fostered a strong sense of belonging. The problem was that the allies would remember the Germans who roamed the Atlantic in packs of U-Boats, and those memories would still be vivid.

"What's the mission, Sir?" he asked the captain hopefully.

"We head east then south. There is a mass-gathering of the dead ones who are going to cut off the retreat of our allies. For whatever reason, their mission cannot fail, so we are to attack the rear of the enemy."

"And then?" Beck asked.

"And then we have to kill them all, I imagine."

———

"Receiving, go ahead," Captain Palmer said into the radio after command insisted on speaking to the officer commanding the convoy. He frowned, his eyebrows meeting at odd angles as his face gave an unfamiliar betrayal for a man who almost always maintained his professional visage.

"Time to intercept?" he asked, flickering his eyes between his watch and the map on the wall in front of his SSM.

"Shit," he swore to himself, undetected by anyone inside the rolling armour, before transmitting on the radio again, "Understood. Out."

He switched channels, transmitting the order to press on with as much speed as possible.

Ahead, at the tip of their column, Maxwell's Spartan chose that exact moment to emit a loud clattering noise and judder to a tortured stop, causing the wagon behind theirs to hit them hard in the rear and concertina the entire column to a very badly timed halt.

———

Peter had told Amber to hide behind the big chair, told her to stay quiet and out of sight as the noises upstairs grew louder. He ran on small, light feet to the bottom of the stairs to wait the tense moments for the sounds of a moving corpse to reach the top and begin their halting descent to where their instinctive brain heard noises. Those noises denoted food, and food drove the thing's feet to move and propel it towards that stimulus.

Peter hid behind the tiny protection of the interior wall to be out of sight of whatever was coming and listened intently, trying to hear over the unnaturally loud sound of his own breathing. The footsteps came steadily, rhythmically, as though the creature coming down the staircase was an actual person in full control of their body, and not the shambolic, jerky actions of a zombie. This realisation made Peter relax and straighten slightly, drawing in a breath to call out a hello. That breath caught in his throat as a new noise drifted around the lower part of the house; that of a gargling, throaty hiss.

At once he knew he had made a mistake. A dangerous

mistake, and one that he made because his focus was on the little girl and not on himself. He had never managed to corner himself in a house with one of the faster ones. In fact, he had only encountered them twice and one of those times he had been forced to use the sawn-off shotgun to decapitate the thing. His eyes flashed left to the door, then straight ahead to the chair that Amber was hiding behind, before looking back towards the door. His brain calculated the distances, the time it would take to get her and get out, and his heart dropped in his chest to know that there was no way to get out.

Unthinkingly, he acted as instinctively as the thing coming to investigate their noise and smell.

"Amber! Run, now! Go!" he shouted, his final word becoming drowned out by the ear-shattering screech coming from just the other side of the thin plasterboard wall.

Amber ran, her small feet slipping on the floor and losing her a precious split-second head start. Peter watched her run, his breath held and his mouth open, then his terror doubled in intensity as he realised the one fact he hadn't accounted for in his escape plan for her.

She reached the door, jumped up and dragged her small fingertips off the locking latch to make it snap back loudly against its spring. The door stayed stubbornly shut and she spun to press her back hard up against the door in paralysing fear as the zombie had emerged from the staircase and locked its clouded eyeballs on her miniature frame and mirrored her wide eyes with its dead ones.

The baggy, pinstriped trousers still had the black and white chequered shirt tucked in, the raised collar skewed and crumpled on one side where a chunk of neck was missing below the floppy mess of unnaturally blonde hair.

Ashen grey lips peeled back from black gums to reveal the contrast of overly-white teeth, and the room filled with the musty smell of old, dry body as it coiled its muscles and bound forward.

The smell was the last straw for Peter.

That instant transportation back to a life which he saw as more dangerous, more claustrophobic and more terrible than the one he now lived, that smell of stale alcohol that made his mind see the woman he hated so much and had killed, but still felt cursed to his very soul for doing so. The memory of his mother made his body move before his mind even processed the emotions.

His mouth opened to emit a strangled cry of fear and rage as his hands came up bearing the pitchfork, which he instinctively aimed at the base of the zombie's skull. His legs propelled him towards it with a few short steps before his left foot stretched out exaggeratedly to provide the thrust with the instinctive power it needed to penetrate the flesh and sinew and save them both.

As that foot went forward to drive his body weight into the killing blow, his toes caught on the corner of the rug and pitched him downwards instead of up.

TWENTY-THREE

Palmer was bombarded with information via radio, learning for the first time that the stranded convoy was directly in the path of a swarm bigger than the one that had formed in the city, and double the size of the one they had encountered a few weeks before, during the battle of the bridge. That information made the confident young officer's face go more than a little pale and sagged his posture. Johnson watched from the corner of his eye as he pretended to study the map wall before him, noting that the captain's right hand was trembling.

The tremble was small, but evidently uncontrollable. Deciding not to wait for the intelligence to come to him second-hand, he switched the channel of his own headset to listen in to the conversation. Hadlington's precise but peevish voice filled his headphones and a surreptitious glance at Daniels on the radio beside him showed that the corporal was also listening. Catching Johnson's disapproving eye, he subtly switched back to the convoy channel and listened to the organisation of Maxwell as he cleared out the obstruction to assess the mechanical failure of his own wagon.

"We are pending approval for helicopter rescue, and other

armoured resources are on their way to you from your north west," Hadlington reported, leaving out the somewhat salient fact that there would not be sufficient helicopters to extract the entire force, "We estimate that your time until interception is less than an hour, if you can get moving immediately."

Palmer's eyes flickered again over the map, figuring out where the convoy would be at that time. He didn't like his estimate.

"Wait one," he said into the radio and turned to Johnson.

"One hour from here puts us where, SSM?"

Johnson already knew the answer, just as Palmer did.

"It puts us at or near the island. Too close for comfort," he said solemnly.

"So we risk endangering the lives of everyone there," Palmer thought out loud.

"ETA for aircraft extraction for precious cargo?" he asked into the radio.

"Three-five, thirty-five minutes, over," came the response. Captain and Squadron Sergeant Major looked at one another and exchanged a silent moment of understanding. The mission. The lives of everyone on the island. Undeniably more important to the bigger picture than their small detachment. Johnson nodded to the officer, who swallowed and transmitted again.

"Send helicopter evac," he said, "convoy will stay in the open so as not to bring the swarm to your location. Out."

———

The noise that four Leopard 2 tanks made, rolling over the M4 motorway bridge spanning the River Severn, was stunning. They pushed hard, demonstrating that they controlled one of the fastest main battle tanks on the planet at the time, and stopped outside Bristol to refuel from the large wagon following them. The troop had brought their entire fighting strength as well as their own replenishments, and Wolff thought it infinitely more sensible to pause and refuel before they came within sight and smell of the enemy.

Turning south and avoiding the sprawling city entirely, they rolled onwards, encountering larger concentrations of shambling zombies as they progressed. These walking corpses weren't always walking; some crawled with damaged or missing legs, others hobbled onwards with mechanical injuries which slowed them down too much to keep up with the main herd that couldn't be seen yet. The only indication that they were ahead was the distant cloud of dust that marked the southern horizon, kicked up by so many thousand pairs of feet, all trudging onwards with some as yet unfathomed common purpose.

Hauptmann Wolff, captain of the troop and breaking convention by commanding the leading tank, told his men to ignore the stragglers and press on through them to the main body of the enemy. Pressing on through, quite literally, the support truck following on behind the tanks drove over swathes of oily mess caused by the crushed bodies, and the men in the passenger seats of those trucks took only necessary shots from their G3 assault rifles against those zombies that posed a threat to them. The men in the tanks ahead had no space for the long rifles, so instead carried Uzi machine pistols for personal defence, should they need to dismount. Their main tool for dispatching the massed dead would be their main 120mm guns and the canister rounds they carried.

When the stragglers became an obstacle in themselves, Wolff scanned the ground ahead for a space wide enough to spread his tanks out and bring their four guns to bear on the mass, which was already beginning to take an interest in the sound and movement behind it. Having thought ahead in his own analytical way, Wolff ordered the four tanks to halt and disperse, then load high explosive rounds into their guns. Unlike their British allies, they didn't have to follow the projectile with a full bag charge for maximum effect and range, as they had the more advanced single-piece ammunition which made their rate of fire slightly superior. He planned to stall the massive crowd with four large explosions, and make them the centre of attention to divert their collective attention back north instead of south, where his orders had informed him they must be prevented from doing so.

"Halt," he called into the radio in their native language, waiting as his next orders were followed and the tanks dispersed into a loose lateral line, "targets to your front. Fire."

Four huge, concussive booms rolled out over the lush landscape, answered by the responding explosions of their high-yield munitions as four brilliant fireballs erupted in the distance.

"Now," Wolff said seriously into the radio, "we have their attention." The men in his own tank smiled, as he hoped the others would be doing.

"Load with canister, staggered fire by numbers, stand by," he ordered in crisply efficient German, watching as his own loader opened the breech and slid in the munition, which appeared the same as a very large bullet. The other tanks reported ready to fire, and Wolff ordered them to illuminate their headlights and fire smoke grenades on his instruction.

"Deploy smoke screen in three, two, one, *fire!*"

As one, the northern skyline from the perspective of the zombies erupted with a series of eight pops to gout billowing smoke. Almost the rear third of the huge gathering had already turned to investigate the explosions, and perhaps a further ten percent of them now responded to the smoke screen display, to hiss and screech as they turned to investigate.

"Canister to your front at intervals," Wolff said calmly, "on my mark."

Then came the agonising wait as the zombies had to be allowed time to approach for their evil and destructive munitions to be fully effective. Wolff watched through his optics, gauging the moment to be just right, and fired the first round himself from his commander's override controls.

The muzzle of their long gun erupted in smoke and flame, recoiling violently to spew the contents of the canister directly into the path of the oncoming horde. The weapon itself, although modernised and made more lethal over time, had not changed much since its inception some time in the sixteenth century. Deployed against infantry, it was brutally effective as instead of firing single projectiles, the canister disintegrated as it was fired and spread the contents of hundreds of tungsten bolts towards the enemy, and it then fanned out to wreak havoc and death like a hideous and gigantic shotgun.

The four rounds of canister were fired in staggered intervals in order that a fresh wave of dead filled the front rank before the next shot was sent out, and not wasted into already ruined bodies. It fanned outwards to rip bloody holes through the first three or four ranks, before the kinetic energy of their multiple projectiles was spent.

The tanks fired with their barrel only slightly elevated past the horizontal, as their expected advance would bring them perilously close to the maximum depression of the barrels and force a retreat in order to keep them at bay. Their coaxial MG3 machine guns could be brought to bear in closer quarters, but sustained fire with these guns had proved to require a change of barrels after an uncomfortably short time in comparison to the British alternative in their GPMG. Of all the NATO countries, most had dropped the use of canister anti-infantry ammunition in favour of the armour-killing sabot kinetic rounds, or armour piercing munitions developed to beat the improved armour of the Russian T-80 main battle tank. The Germans' reluctance to withdraw that ammunition had been a fortuitous advantage against their unexpected enemy.

Wave after wave of the dead fell in bloody ruin as great gouts of red mist filled the air above their shattered and dismembered bodies. Some unlucky ones nearer the front caught multiple pieces of the machined shrapnel and seemed to simply disintegrate as parts of their bodies vanished under the onslaught of metal.

Round after round they fired, each report attracting more and more of the undead to turn and investigate the sounds, but the simple mathematics of the equation had never been in their favour. As devastating as their combined firepower was, as many shattered and ruined bodies they threw back with each efficient shot, the tide turned against them.

"Back, back!" Wolff called over the radio as his gunner fired their last shot at maximum depression. The tanks began to roll backwards to bring the front ranks back into their killing fields, but the progress only ramped higher in intensity as the faster ones towards the front of the horde forced their way through to the rear, and pressed out ahead of the mass.

Wolff engaged the MG under his control, barking out rapid bursts of heavy machine gun fire at the smooth motorway tarmac at the feet of the faster ones, for the bullets to bounce back up and graze along, cutting off legs and shattering ankles to stop the advance. Faster they reversed, outpacing the attack and firing relentlessly with all four big smoothbore guns spitting metal and death, as their accompanying twin machine guns rattled away at the enemy.

The tide turned in favour of the living as that fresh wave went down and the slower ones following their lead were forced to climb over the mound of dead that marked the limit of the guns. The tanks pressed forwards, elevating their barrels to scour the lip of that barrier of dead flesh, to be scattered away until the skyline ahead was suddenly empty.

They had attacked the horde, laid bloody ruin to so many thousands of them and formed a wall ten feet high and three times as deep, with more bodies than any of them could possibly imagine.

And they had still only killed less than a quarter of them.

TWENTY-FOUR

Lieutenant Commander Murray of Her Majesty's Royal Navy shouted at his support crew to hurry because he needed to be in the air ten minutes ago.

He began his pre-flight checks, whipping through them at reckless speed, before the aircraft had even been fully refuelled. The split-second he got a raised thumb from the helmeted man on the ground, he yanked on the controls hard to force the unnatural flying machine vertically skywards, before rotating to somewhere vaguely resembling his bearing and tilting the bulbous nose down to blast away in that direction.

He had left the argument raging in the headquarters building, with that frustratingly punctilious Major wanting to know precise fuel usage and carrying weights before he would authorise any mission. Barret, the senior of the two naval pilots, opened a debate regarding seniority, if only to defer attention as Murray sprinted towards his helicopter with the coordinates scribbled hastily onto a scrap of paper. The army major brought in the army colonel, who of course wanted to know the whole story from the beginning and to congratulate people on a fine presentation, as though lives weren't at stake. Barret fed wood into that fire as he argued with Hadlington, until everyone in the room froze at the sound of helicopter engines screaming inland over their heads.

Barret feigned a look of confusion and asked the room who the devil that could be flying over their airspace. He gave his excuses and said that he would check that none of his men knew anything about it, leaving colonel Tim Munro smiling up at Hadlington. The major didn't know if that was out of mirth that the men of the Fleet Air Arm had blatantly disregarded his instructions, or whether in fact the old man even knew what had just happened.

"Major, allow me to tell you a brief anecdote from my school days," he said as he leaned back and seemed to melt into nostalgia, "I was at Gordonstoun with His Royal Highness," he said wistfully, as most of his stories began, "although he was younger than I by a few years. I recall it was a spring time affair," he chuckled suddenly, "but then again, a Highlands spring time would freeze you southern folk to your chairs, and we were given a hearty run over the moors. We all agreed to take a shortcut and slow down our progress to give the appearance that we had run the full circuit despite the godawful weather. When we got back, maintaining a good ruse as we staggered our returns, each boy was congratulated for their time and rewarded with hot porridge," he finished, smiling up at Hadlington, and having that smile echoed by the young Lieutenant who followed the Colonel everywhere.

"And, Sir?" Hadlington asked impatiently, waiting with as much grace as he could before his annoyance overcame his manners.

"And, Major," Colonel Tim said ruefully, "sometimes it's best not to notice when folk don't follow your orders when you realise it was unreasonable to expect that from them in the first place."

With that he smiled, stood, replaced his uniform cap and

strolled off in the direction of the bridge to inspect the men as though on garrison duty in some pleasant foreign posting.

————

Murray screamed his helicopter low and hard across the landscape. His anger at the ridiculous order came out through the controls as he did the helicopter pilot equivalent of driving angry. Even if they had half a dozen Sea Kings, they would barely be able to withdraw the men of the convoy, so the lack of their second aircraft on the rescue mission made little to no difference.

Hadlington had been waiting for permission to send the aircraft, and that permission was pending the outcome of the allied attack on the swarm of dead. No update had come, either from the tank platoon themselves or the reconnaissance planes flying high above, and so Hadlington had lacked the flexibility to pre-empt the order from command and deploy a helicopter.

As secret as the information had been, soldiers talking about a potential cure had tongues wagging all over the island.

Surely, Murray had thought to himself, *any potential cure is worth investing everything we have into recovering it?*

Shaking away his annoyance and incomprehension at the rigidity and stubbornly bureaucratic nature of the armed forces, he continued making his way towards the convoy, while behind him the first of the heavy shore bombardment began to land.

————

"Helicopter inbound," Palmer said to his troopers, who had mostly dismounted to assist stripping the crippled Spartans at their front. Maxwell's in the lead had suffered a total mechanical failure and would not engage any gear either forwards or backwards, and the one behind would need three men working with sledgehammers for an hour to straighten out the bent metal and allow the tracks to move unimpeded. Palmer had decided to forget trying to bring them home and instead ordered as much ammunition out of those wagons, and the men to squeeze in wherever they could find safe space inside the armour.

When they had stopped, the rear sections of the Saxons had swung open and the bewildered civilian in a very dirty white coat was unceremoniously bundled into the compartment, along with the box that the two special forces teams had recovered. One team sealed themselves up tightly again to protect the man and his items, and the others had spread out into the bushes on all four compass points.

The Sea King was audible long before it was visible, and Palmer ordered some of his troopers to secure the patch of flat grass fifty metres away from where their wagons were stopped. The aircraft swooped in as the four bearded men with their modern weaponry emerged out of cover again and opened the rear of the Saxon to form a bubble of eight armed soldiers around the man in their centre. He was transported as though swept along by armoured beetles, deposited into the belly of the helicopter, and then Palmer watched a very brief conversation of shouts and sign language take place between the soldiers.

"You go," bawled Downes to Bufford, "you're going straight out to sea anyway, and that's your remit. Not ours."

Buffs leaned back, regarding the SAS Major carefully before nodding once and signalling his men to climb aboard. He thought through the suggestion, weighing up the pros and cons of the concept, then decided that it was a tactical decision to send the SBS out to sea and keep the SAS on dry land, and nothing to do with organisational egotism. Bufford snatched four spare magazines for his MP5, all fully loaded. Seeing what he was doing and understanding immediately, his three men did the same and pressed the additional firepower onto the SAS men, who gave them grateful nods.

Their new rule on ammunition against this unexpected enemy was the same as their personal mantra for explosives; P for Plenty.

As the four former Royal Marines climbed up, the others ducked low to retreat from the rotor wash and just as soon as it arrived, the helicopter was gone. They jogged back to the armour without a second glance at the aircraft that could have whisked them out of the country to safety, to find Captain Palmer whipping up his men into fearsome activity.

"Come on, let's move!" he shouted, before he saw the major and leaned over his open hatch to shout to him over the sound of engines sparking into noisy life.

"The swarm hasn't been stopped, and they're still heading for the island," he said simply. Without another word the SAS men filed back into the rear of their Saxon as the other was filled with men and spare ammunition. Mac paused only briefly to pick up the dismounted GPMG from one of the Spartans and give a nod to Dezzy to collect the link ammunition for it. Engines revved, and the reduced convoy headed towards their temporary home with the seemingly hopeless intention of preventing its being overrun.

———

The twin Mk45 127mm guns of the American Destroyer began pounding as soon as they came in range of the horde. Their heavy artillery shells soared high over the coastline to rocket inland and fall amongst the mass of bodies, startling everyone on the island. Their update via Commander Briggs had been that the tanks had intercepted the swarm and inflicted heavy casualties, but had floundered after they had been unable to continue their pursuit due to the piles of dead they had created. Forced to find an alternative route, their German allies were effectively out of the game.

The convoy, no longer carrying the precious cargo after a Royal Navy pilot had pulled them out of the flames, was also making its way towards the island, hoping to hit the horde of enemy in their flank.

The captain of the ship saw no other way that the day could be won, so he ordered his ship to be brought up to the shore and for their guns to be unleashed as soon as they were in range. The only thing he wouldn't do was use the Tomahawk cruise missiles, following the presidential decree that they should not be used without direct White House authorisation. But that didn't stop him getting his deck guns in the fight.

Each huge round falling on the crowd did untold damage to those zombies in the immediate area of the splash and explosion, but every crater created by the big guns was instantly filled with the rolling mass of bodies, and each shot fell closer to the island as the targeting was adjusted.

Briggs initially couldn't understand why there was a seemingly pathological need to attack the swarm instead of letting it dissipate, as most of the others had done. This especially seeing as the island was no longer tactically important to the overall parameters of success, now that the contents of the London laboratory had been recovered, and he carefully offered that opinion to the captain.

"They've all gotta be killed at some point, right?" he responded with detached glee, "may as well do it now when the sons-of-bitches decided to have a civil rights march!"

Briggs, as cold as he was, found the excitement for taking even formerly-human life with such reckless overkill distasteful.

And so it became a countdown.

The swarm stepped closer to the island each minute, and

each minute the guns of the destroyer degraded them further, until such time as the German tanks and the Brits in their armoured cars caught up with them and added their own hail of ammunition to the party.

Which, after just under an hour, was what happened.

Just as the leading edge of the swarm came into sight, the two Chieftain tanks opened up directly into them with round after round. Every Fox car had been parked where their 30mm Rarden cannons could be brought to bear, and their speed-loaders stacked with six heavy shots ready to pour into the enemy. At the distances they could see on the island, their shot would not fall, because they were firing at less than two miles away. Every elevated section of the island that had line of sight on the single approach road rained down artillery on the smudge of approaching death, and none of them had resorted to using their machine guns yet as the distance was still too great. When their enemy grew closer to under a mile away, then the belt-fed machine guns would spark into life and provide a constant and persistent clattering din to overpower all but the biggest of the explosions.

Palmer's convoy arrived just as the vanguard of dead began breaking away to sprint ahead for the bridge, and their mounted guns rolled lead and tracer and the promise of a second, more permanent death.

The German heavy tanks, unable to find a suitable route to catch up, despite their superior road speed for such large beasts, were twenty minutes too late to prevent disaster.

TWENTY-FIVE

Peter pitched forward in slow motion, his brain telling him the gruesome outcome before he had even hit the carpeted floor of the living room.

He knew that Amber would be bitten, her young skin would be torn and would bleed, and he would hear her screams before he could get back to his feet and save her.

He had promised her only a few days before that he would protect her and wouldn't leave her, and now his eyes pricked with tears as he fell, because he knew the last thing he would see and hear before he died was the little girl being torn apart.

That fear and desperation became resolve as he flailed about to try and recover his trip, which had only partly distracted the zombie from flying at the girl. That desperate resolve manifested itself into a blind thrust of the pitchfork in his flailing right hand which bit into the fleshy back of the creature with little force and struck bone straight away.

Peter knew even as his face hit the plush carpet that he had failed her, because hitting bone usually meant that the things just carried on as though nothing had happened to them.

Confusingly for Peter, the sound of him hitting the floor

sounded much louder and later than his brain expected, and he opened his eyes to see the feet of the zombie just in front of his nose. Leaping to his feet, he threw himself backwards and scrabbled for the spike he had sheathed on his right hip and held it out towards the twitching thing lying face down.

He saw the single bare foot, purple and bloated from the blood that had pooled there when it died, and the other foot inexplicably covered by a brown sock, and he watched as the bare foot twitched again as though electrocuted. He got to his feet and stepped carefully closer, sparing a quick glance to Amber to see that she was staring at it with her head cocked in confusion. Peter kept the spike held in both hands, levelled at the prone monstrosity as he shuffled around out of its reach to get to her, and then he saw exactly what she could see.

The zombie was trying to claw its way towards her, using only its head and neck as its teeth sank into the heavy pile of the carpet, making the attempts to drag itself forward both fruitless and pathetic. He relaxed and stepped closer, seeing his discarded pitchfork lying beside the crippled zombie and a single, dark puncture wound at the base of its neck.

He had no idea how it had happened, but the tip of a single prong on his pitchfork had penetrated the skin and tissue to force its way in between the sixth and seventh bones of the cervical spine and punctured the spinal cord protected inside. He had effectively, and completely accidentally, paralysed their attacker.

The two children stared at it as it tried to reach up for them as though sheer will and determination could make the food come to its mouth. Peter spun the spike in his hand and walked around to the back of it where he was furthest away from the teeth. Deciding that he preferred to do what he had to do at a distance, he slipped the spike back into his belt, picked up his pitchfork and raised it in both hands before he looked up and saw Amber. He paused, indicating with a flick of his head that she should move and not watch. She shrugged and stepped aside to stand off to his right. With one hard thrust he ended the pitiful attempts of the paralysed zombie to drool him to death.

Their sudden, terrifying fright forgotten, the two children searched the house together and filled the cart with everything they wanted before wheeling it back to their new home. They made two trips back to that house, finding useful items as well as food and drinks, and more ammunition for the shotgun, which Peter took even though he had only ever fired a single shot from the weapon.

They stopped for some food before they abandoned that house as it had been picked clean before moving on to the house opposite. That house was, mercifully, free from zombies. As they were wheeling back their second haul from there, the sounds of rolling thunder began in the far distance.

The thunder sounded in pairs, their echoing twins sounds undulating over and over until replaced by the next wave, to create a rolling wave of ever-increasing intensity until the entire sky was filled with ceaseless noise. Both of them stood still in the road and stared at the empty sky until Peter's nerve broke first.

"Let's get inside," he said softly, reaching down with one empty hand only half thinking about what he was doing.

Just as automatically, Amber reached up and clasped his hand.

The two of them turned and wheeled their piled-up cart back towards their new house and opened the front door. They worked in silence, stacking their haul in the kitchen as the world outside grew even louder, and after they had finished, Amber's face grew dark and worried at the sounds outside. Peter unwrapped chocolate for her in an attempt to take her mind off the growing concern of whatever terrible thing was happening outside. She sat subdued, chewing slowly and visibly upset. Peter racked his brain for what to say to her. He picked up the cassette player and headphones, wasting a few seconds before remembering that the batteries had slowly died the last time he had given it to her. He had yet to find a new tape to go in the player but seeing as she didn't seem to mind the same song, it hadn't been high on his list of priorities when clearing the last few houses. He rummaged around in the kitchen drawer where he had stored the batteries from the houses in that village and found two of the right size before fitting them to the player and taking it over to where she sat quietly. He handed it to her and smiled, seeing her small look of gratitude as she placed the red foam of the flimsy headphones over her ears.

Hearing her hum along to the chorus was the sweetest sound he had ever heard, but it didn't drown out the sounds of what Peter suspected were bombs being dropped not far away. He went to close the small kitchen window in the hope that the sound would be muted, but as he did so the cat emerged from below with a vertical leap which made him jump backwards in fright. His heart beating in his chest, he turned to see if Amber had been frightened by it too, but he saw that she was still engrossed in the music and hadn't turned around. The cat teetered on the threshold for a moment as it eyed him expectantly, then dropped down to meow loudly and rub against his hand, doing the dance it did when asking for food.

Peter wasn't fooled. He knew the cat didn't love him but was only acting so that he worked the can opener. But in that same moment, he realised that he was fine being used by the animal just because it had decided to stay around them and because it made Amber happy.

He fed the cat first, then made them something to eat before joining her on the comfortable chairs where she sat listening to music and playing with the small plastic figures he had found before they had met.

———

High on the cliffs looking out over a misty English Channel, two men ran into the main hall of the old building, wearing looks of fear and confusion. The man in charge, who had only called himself Michaels to them, seemed unconcerned and that made them feel instantly foolish. He didn't get up, merely lounged in a chair, smoking and looking out to sea through the big picture windows.

"Yes?" he asked, knowing what they wanted but making them feel like scared children for asking.

"That noise?" one of them asked timidly, hoping that the rest would be obvious.

"What of it?"

"What… er… what is it? Please?" said the other one as he wrung his hands and seemed unable to stand still.

"That, gentlemen," Michaels said as he swung his legs down and stood abruptly, "is the sound of heavy guns. Some way away, I imagine, and nothing to bother us here. Anything else?"

There wasn't, and he invited them kindly to fuck off and leave him be.

In the hotel erected next to the grand building, two women sat with wide eyes as they listened to what sounded like the result of angering the weather gods raging in the skies of the south coast.

———

"Automatic fire, to your front, go on," Captain Palmer said unnecessarily, as the ragged remains of his overfilled convoy tore into the left flank of the massive horde of zombies. They were just out of sight of the island itself, but not of their effective fire, which tore great holes into the attack from their oblique angle.

Palmer and Johnson were the only men in the convoy not closed down, as their vehicle was the only one bearing a weapon that could not be fired from inside. The Saxons were little more than armoured trucks designed to keep their occupants safe from enemy fire, and they were set back to the rear. Palmer didn't fire the machine gun because it was at the limit of effective fire and the 30mm cannons on the Fox cars were lethal at that range, as they pumped shot after shot indiscriminately into the crowd.

Both officer and SSM watched the fall of shot as the battle raged ahead, both noticing the regular timing between the huge splash damage of heavier munitions than they carried.

"Your Chieftains?" Johnson asked Palmer, knowing the answer was a negative as soon as he had said it, but failing to come up with an alternative explanation.

"No," Palmer said, "bigger, must be the n…"

"Shore bombardment," Johnson exclaimed loudly over the noise of the battle raging around them as he finally understood what he was seeing.

"Must be five- or six-inch guns," Palmer said.

"Nice," Johnson said, with evil relish in response to one of those naval guns firing a round that exploded and sent body parts cartwheeling impossibly high into the air.

"Press on?" he asked the officer, suggesting in that senior NCO manner that the officer needed a reminding nudge. Palmer picked up the handset and keyed the radio to respond.

"Advance one hundred."

The armour lurched forward, closer to the moving river of dead flesh and rendering it that much clearer to their eyes.

"Christ on a fucking bike," Johnson said in horror as the sheer scale of the swarm was made clear to him, then he ducked back inside and hoisted up his sub-machine gun as reassurance.

"Indeed, Mister Johnson," Palmer responded with his usual impeccable manners, "I just hope our chaps back at base are doing alright."

"They haven't got near the bridge yet," Johnson reassured him, pointing towards the mess of nothingness and meat ahead of them.

———

With no clear commander at the bridge, the men performed their own tasks in crews or troops or sections as they saw fit. The two tanks, one blocking the road and the other firing at a gentle angle from a piece of flat ground to the side of the road-way, poured a hideously destructive amount of fire into the oncoming enemy, who seemed only able to manage progress of an inch at a time. Added to that the combined weight of every Fox car they had left, pouring 30mm rounds into the attack, and over a dozen belt-fed heavy machine guns blasting a storm of lead from their chattering barrels.

Peculiar pops and thuds sounded occasionally as three 51mm mortars were served effectively by the one crew left behind from assault troop and two teams of Marines. Those rounds were a mixture of high explosive and smoke, not for the vision screen but for their incendiary properties of the white phosphorous fillers. Flaming zombies occasionally emerged from the smoke as is was whipped away by the strong wind for them to be blasted apart by high explosive or else cut down by varying degrees of direct fire.

The barrels of the Chieftain tanks were fully depressed by then and unable to bring their muzzles to bear on the leading edge of the attack, instead concentrating on the lowest depression they could manage to degrade the enemy attack as best they could.

On the slopes above them, Major Hadlington tried desperately to call in air support for the beleaguered defenders, as he saw no way to survive the unstoppable invasion, and almost lost the power of speech when he considered that the swarm had initially been almost thirty percent bigger. He had tried to order the Royal Navy helicopter to take off and repeat their trick with the music but Lieutenant Commander Barrett was adamant that everyone, and he included the surprise shore bombardment in that list, would have to stop firing for long enough for them to take off and hover in close to the swarm to lead them away like the pied piper a second time. That pause would result in the bridge being overrun.

Command were unwavering as they denied his repeated requests for airstrikes, as he was told over and over to wait and that there were higher priorities, until eventually they stopped answering his hails.

And then, even the shore bombardment stopped, but not before one last errant round changed their situation for the worse.

———

"Understood," the captain said to the bridge after receiving the orders to cease fire and withdraw to deeper water, "gunners, cease fire, cease fire. Helm, take us about due west."

The gunners fired their final shot and powered down the huge deck guns as the ship's engines powered up to steam them out into the mouth of the Atlantic.

Nobody asked the question about their sudden breaking off from the attack, but the captain answered the thoughts anyway.

"Ours is not to make reply, ours is not to reason why…" he said with melodic sadness.

———

The final two 127mm high-yield explosive rounds left the long barrels of the deck guns at an impossible velocity and arced their way over the grey water. They were still over the steely waves of the English Channel when they began their long descent towards the target, unseen and in the far distance from where the projectile had started its journey.

These last, lonely rounds were fired as the ship had already begun to turn, dipping the nose of the vessel just enough to change the course of history as the effect on the shot caused them to fall low and miss the zombies.

What they did hit, and in spectacular fashion, was the concrete support beam of the elevated section of the causeway and it caused a shudder to run through the entire length of the bridge. Huge chunks of rock and concrete spewed upwards high into the air, scattering body parts even higher and scattering them over the roadblock.

Cracks appeared in the road, the sound of splitting concrete so loud that it was audible over the gunfire, and Horton felt his stomach lurch inside the closed-down tank weighing in at a shade under fifty-four tonnes.

As one, the three men of the four-man crew housed inside the turret froze as their inner-ear warned them of something more terrible than the approaching horde. There was time for Horton to say one single word before the tank lurched and dropped half a foot as the first part of the degraded bridge began to give.

"Fuck!"

Horton and the loader below and beside him shot their hands up to reach the handles to open the hatches. Millward,

Horton's gunner sitting ahead and below him, crabbed backwards and upwards so unbelievably fast that he climbed backwards over Horton to get out of the hatch before he could, but as he hauled himself out to lead for the roadway, ten feet behind him the concrete cracked again and the tank he leapt from vanished straight downwards.

Sinking immediately in the fifteen feet of water below, Horton lay flat on his chest and screamed "No," at the shimmering sight of his tank under the water. Bubbles rose as the tanks moved, crabbing slightly sideways as the driver, trapped in the forward compartment and closed down, threw the beast into reverse and gunned the engine only to flood it with water after six feet of underwater travel. Horton watched, willing the man to open the forward hatch and swim to safety, but nothing happened. Standing to strip his webbing off, he was hauled to the ground by Millward, his gunner, who told him over and over again that he was gone.

He was gone, but the forty-foot long section of the bridge that had taken him down had also prevented the swarm from getting any closer as they piled endlessly into the water to be swept away by the strong current in the direction of the wind.

Gun and cannon fire still rained down on the swarm, but the damage had been done. Their forces were split and scattered, and events in the wider world had just taken a turn to make their small corner of Britain utterly irrelevant.

EPILOGUE

Thousands of miles west, alarms had sounded, and red lights flashed in a dozen underground control rooms all over the United States. Orders were shouted, and urgent telephone calls were made.

One of those calls was placed directly to the White House and interrupted the President's lunch.

"Sir, they've launched," said the voice. The president's face dropped. He half expected, and half hoped that this time would never come. The 'they' part of the single sentence was as obvious as the thing that had been launched.

Decades of conditioning, years of expecting the worst and mentally preparing for the day when the hard decision would have to be made meant that when the time actually came, he didn't hesitate.

"Launch counter-strikes," he said, giving his authentication before replacing the telephone in the cradle, "and may God have mercy on our souls," he added to nobody in particular.

———

Silo doors opened, and rockets ignited, just as had happened in three locations in the Soviet Union. Their missiles, however, were aimed at levelling the remaining undead population of continental Europe to zero to prevent the endless waves of attack on their borders. Those launches had been detected in the west, and the counter-strikes had launched before their nukes had landed in Europe.

Despite the two huge nations being on the verge of war with each other, they still enjoyed direct contact between their governments, where nobody would ever be left on hold.

Calls were placed, desperately asking for the launches to be aborted. Arguments raged, threats were levelled, and time was wasted.

The nukes landed in Europe, closely followed by the six tactical strikes on military and government sites all over Russia. Despite the threats, the retaliatory strikes didn't come, and the US forces sailed away west to abandon Europe and the UK.

The British were on their own, and the list of priorities was so long that the fates of a scattered mixed unit of military and two small orphans with their cat didn't even feature.

FROM THE PUBLISHER

Thank you for reading *Aftermath,* the second of six books in Toy Soldiers.

We hope you enjoyed it as much as we enjoyed bringing it to you. We just wanted to take a moment to encourage you to review the book on Amazon and Goodreads. Every review helps further the author's reach and, ultimately, helps them continue writing fantastic books for us all to enjoy.

If you liked this book, check out the rest of our catalogue at www.aethonbooks.com. To sign up to receive a FREE collection from some of our best authors as well as updates regarding all new releases, visit www.aethonbooks.com/sign-up

SPECIAL THANKS TO:

ADAWIA E. ASAD
JENNY AVERY
BARDE PRESS
CALUM BEAULIEU
BEN
BECKY BEWERSDORF
BHAM
TANNER BLOTTER
ALFRED JOSEPH BOHNE IV
CHAD BOWDEN
ERREL BRAUDE
DAMIEN BROUSSARD
CATHERINE BULLINER
JUSTIN BURGESS
MATT BURNS
BERNIE CINKOSKE
MARTIN COOK
ALISTAIR DILWORTH
JAN DRAKE
BRET DULEY
RAY DUNN
ROB EDWARDS
RICHARD EYRES
MARK FERNANDEZ
CHARLES T FINCHER
SYLVIA FOIL
GAZELLE OF CAERBANNOG
DAVID GEARY
MICHEAL GREEN
BRIAN GRIFFIN

EDDIE HALLAHAN
JOSH HAYES
PAT HAYES
BILL HENDERSON
JEFF HOFFMAN
GODFREY HUEN
JOAN QUERALTÓ IBÁÑEZ
JONATHAN JOHNSON
MARCEL DE JONG
KABRINA
PETRI KANERVA
ROBERT KARALASH
VIKTOR KASPERSSON
TESLAN KIERINHAWK
ALEXANDER KIMBALL
JIM KOSMICKI
FRANKLIN KUZENSKI
MEENAZ LODHI
DAVID MACFARLANE
JAMIE MCFARLANE
HENRY MARIN
CRAIG MARTELLE
THOMAS MARTIN
ALAN D. MCDONALD
JAMES MCGLINCHEY
MICHAEL MCMURRAY
CHRISTIAN MEYER
SEBASTIAN MÜLLER
MARK NEWMAN
JULIAN NORTH

KYLE OATHOUT
LILY OMIDI
TROY OSGOOD
GEOFF PARKER
NICHOLAS (BUZ) PENNEY
JASON PENNOCK
THOMAS PETSCHAUER
JENNIFER PRIESTER
RHEL
JODY ROBERTS
JOHN BEAR ROSS
DONNA SANDERS
FABIAN SARAVIA
TERRY SCHOTT
SCOTT
ALLEN SIMMONS
KEVIN MICHAEL STEPHENS
MICHAEL J. SULLIVAN
PAUL SUMMERHAYES
JOHN TREADWELL
CHRISTOPHER J. VALIN
PHILIP VAN ITALLIE
JAAP VAN POELGEEST
FRANCK VAQUIER
VORTEX
DAVID WALTERS JR
MIKE A. WEBER
PAMELA WICKERT
JON WOODALL
BRUCE YOUNG

9 781949 890358